UNDERCOVER SECRETS, UNTOLD LIES

by

Jasmine Austin Moore

Bella
BOOKS

2013

Bella Books, Inc.
P.O. Box 10543
Tallahassee, FL 32302

Printed in the United States of America on acid-free paper
First published 2013

Cover Designer: Judith Fellows

ISBN 13: 978-1-59493-336-3

Dedication

I would like to thank all the important women in my life who have supported me, especially PDM who read, edited and shared ideas; Karen who brainstormed over many breakfasts; and my wonderful partner in crime, PJ, who has always offered encouragement. Thank you to my editor, Karin, Linda, Jessica and all the other wonderful people at Bella Books. A special thanks to my awesome mother, who has supported me in all life's adventures.

About the Author

As an longtime teddy bear collector, with a collection nearing museum proportions, I always have plenty of company during the many long hours of writing.

CHAPTER ONE

Gwen Meyers slid behind the two police cruisers, parking her Crown Vic just an inch from the back bumper of one of the black-and-whites. Damn, the road was slippery. She had thought, no, had honestly hoped and prayed, that the snow was over for the season after the welcome February thaw. The snowbanks had just melted down to a manageable level when northern Wisconsin got hit hard again with another six inches. Today's snowstorm was mixed with freezing ice and hail. She left her car running with the window defroster on full blast so she wouldn't have to chisel ice off her windshield later. She zipped up her parka and stuffed her hands into her gloves as she slid out of the car into the frigid air.

"Morning, Detective." Officer Jenny O'Neil walked toward her with a grim expression plastered on her face. "It's a bad one."

"What have you got so far?" Gwen asked, watching three cops traipsing down the steep incline while red and blue lights bounced off the white landscape like a kaleidoscope. She could smell the distinctive scent of death from up here, even with the stiff northerly wind gusting angrily.

"Looks like she lost control around the bend. Car must have bounced a couple times down the ravine before ending up overturned in old man Kaplan's cow pasture. He's the one who called it in."

"Hey, it's Kathy Wright!" Scott Richards called up.

Gwen all but reeled from shock.

"Shit!" Gwen managed to exclaim. "The captain's daughter! Don't publicize the identity over the police band. When he finds out his only daughter is dead, he'll be right here on the scene. Let's get the crime techs down here first. Jenny, call it in on your cell instead of the police band. I'm going down."

Gwen maintained her tough demeanor, trying desperately not to show how upset she was. She turned away and stomped off, angrily swiping away a tear with her gloved hand, and tried to convince herself the bite of cold wind against her exposed flesh was what was making her eyes teary enough to blur her vision.

Walking carefully so she didn't lose her footing, Gwen followed the larger footsteps of the men, trying to step into the deep impressions already made in the snow. About twenty-five feet down the hill she lowered herself next to Scott. The tall sergeant was kneeling over the body that had been ejected from the car. With the hood of his parka pulled tight around his face, he looked like an Eskimo who had just pulled out a whopper fish and thrown it from his ice fishing shanty onto the white tundra.

Scott was a veteran detective, having come up the ranks patrolling the streets, and then spent three grueling years in Vice, mainly busting drug dealers. He was the most gentlemanly, unprejudiced man Gwen had ever met, since most men of his experience were hardened by their constant contact with the unsavory elements of society. Nearly six-two in height, he was thin as a rail and wore his blond hair long, sometimes tying it at the nape of his neck in a ponytail. His kindly smile and friendly outlook belied his tough interior, his being able to get many suspects he interrogated to pour out their life stories. Gwen always thought it was his deep blue, penetrating eyes which made people anxious to confess to him. The thirty-two-year-old had a dry sense of humor and unrelenting determination. All of which she needed now.

Kathy was bloated, her face an ugly purple and green, and she was frozen onto the icy snow.

"She didn't die here," Scott said grimly.

Gwen nodded. Kathy had been dead awhile, possibly as much as three or four days despite the frozen surroundings. Rigor mortis, the chemical changes in the muscles to make them stiffen, was long gone. But why stage an accident and dump the body, knowing the medical examiner would be able to pinpoint the time of death at a much earlier time?

"Hey, there are footprints over here," one of the other officers shouted. "They're moving up the hill away from the scene."

"Throw a shield down to keep them from filling up with snow. Jenny's calling the crime scene unit now," Gwen yelled back.

Kathy Wright was wearing jeans, black, calf-high leather boots, and a tan cable sweater. No coat, hat or gloves. Had she not died from the car accident, she would have surely frozen to death; it wouldn't take long to succumb to exposure in these frigid elements. Gwen stared at the right sleeve of Kathy's sweater, remembering a track of needle marks approximately an inch long in the crook of her arm. She wondered if it was still there. She'd heard Kathy was off drugs after six months in rehab, but couldn't recall if anyone had reported whether she had stayed clean for long. Another tear threatened to fall from Gwen's eyes as she remembered Kathy's painful struggles with addiction.

Gwen knew Kathy and her tragic history well. They'd been friends in high school. Gosh, was that only seven years ago? The spoiled, only child of an educated couple could have had it all. She was tall, five-eleven in her stocking feet, with flowing long blond hair, and a build men turned to stare at whenever she walked down the avenue. She was smart, talented and athletic. Her mom had been a college professor at the local extension and Kathy had a full scholarship to go there as well. The family started falling apart after Kathy's mom had died suddenly of a brain aneurysm. Stanley Wright never could quite accept his wife's death, and had buried himself in his work. He had climbed the ladder quickly in Scarletsville's police department. That left Kathy unattended at seventeen young years of age to experiment with life's most dangerous vices. And experiment she did, whether it was skiing down the steepest slopes, beating the boys on the drag strip in her souped-up Chevy, or drinking everyone else under the table at the local beer halls. She eventually turned to drugs for a faster high.

Kathy had moved out to the capital city, Madison, to attend college after graduation from high school. Gwen was already in the police academy when she had gotten a call from Kathy. She seemed to be happy and enjoying life again, and had invited Gwen to come down for Halloween weekend. It was a fascinating three days, touring the city, window-shopping down State Street, and visiting quaint little pubs that catered to the college crowd. Halloween night had been a blast, with everyone dressed in amazing costumes and parading down the streets. Gwen could describe it only as a block party for five or six thousand of the young, hell-raising residents. She and Kathy had dressed up as jail escapees, with broad black stripes painted across old white medical scrubs, with their legs tied together with a black plastic ball and chain.

Her eyes tearing again, Gwen pushed the memory out of her mind. She would find out what had happened to her former friend and bring to justice whoever was responsible for her death.

CHAPTER TWO

"What have we got?" Gwen asked, looking over her team. They were all huddled around the squad room table with steaming cups of coffee or tea, trying to thaw out from the bitter cold. They'd spent three hours surveying the crime scene and walking the grid around the area, pointing out any scraps of evidence that the crime scene techs could bag and put into the evidence locker.

"Not much." Scott sighed deeply. "The car was wiped clean, and I mean squeaky-clean. Not even Kathy's prints were inside."

Jenny cleared her throat. "We're pulling in every mark we've got. I've already talked to about a dozen of our more reliable informants from the downtown and east side areas where she lived and worked. No one knows a thing. One man said the last time he saw Kathy was about a week ago. He said she bought a bag of meth for fifty dollars and left, but that's not from one of our more 'stable' sources. Most don't recall seeing her for a couple of months."

"Who's in charge here?" The loud, deep, booming voice stopped Jenny from saying anything further. The uniformed man was at least six feet tall, had a short silver-gray crew cut, and carried a sizable paunch that hung grotesquely over his belt. He was shaking with rage.

Gwen remembered meeting Captain Wright several times when she was with Kathy. He was as strict with his daughter as Gwen had heard he was with new recruits, and she cringed at the thought of the angry words Kathy had spoken to lash out in defiance. Perhaps had he been more understanding, Kathy wouldn't have been so anxious to escape through drugs. Gwen swallowed her sorrow as well as the revulsion she felt for this man. She didn't have time for tears now. She had to stay strong for Kathy's sake, and was determined to make finding her killer a personal quest.

"I am," Gwen said confidently after a few moments of stunned silence. "Captain Wright, I'm sorry about your daughter."

"Damn well better be more than sorry, Meyers. I want to get to the bottom of this and right now," Wright snarled. "And keep me informed of every development, do you hear me? No matter how insignificant you may think it is, I want to know!"

"We're doing everything possible," Gwen managed.

"I want to find the bastard that...that..." He sniffed and stifled a sob. "Find him!" he managed, and stormed out of the room.

"For those of you who don't already know," Gwen explained, "Kathy Wright's father is Captain Stanley Wright of North Scarletsville."

"Holy shit," Brad muttered. "He's going to make our investigation that much more difficult. Can you, uh, keep him out of our hair, Gwen?"

Brad could not have been more different than his partner, Scott. Brad was short and stout, compact and muscular. He had boyish good looks and his dark hair was always neatly combed with sweeping bangs and matched in color to a bushy mustache. Gwen often took his joking seriously, as his smile was hidden by the thick growth over his upper lip. It wasn't until she looked at the deep laugh lines around his dark, penetrating eyes that she knew when he was kidding. Having worked on computers since they were first invented, the thirty-six-year-old worked wonders to get information off hard drives, even when they had supposedly been wiped clean.

"I don't know how much influence I'll have," Gwen said honestly. "I knew him pretty well when Kathy and I were in high school, but we've been out of touch for years. I'll do everything I can to keep him from interfering in our investigation." She supposed it would come out that she and Kathy were closer than just high school buddies, but she wasn't ready to divulge that information yet. Her emotions were too raw to talk about it now.

"That's all you can do," Scott said kindly. "I've got the warrant to search Kathy's apartment. Anyone want to come along? The techs should already be on the way."

"I'll go with you," Gwen volunteered. "Jenny, keep up with the drug contacts and see if there's anyone who saw her more recently. Brad, I want that car gone over from top to bottom with a fine-tooth comb. I want any trace hair or fiber analyzed. The perp had to have left something behind. The rest of you start calling her friends, acquaintances, former schoolmates. Someone had to have known who she was hanging with before she died. We'll meet in the morning, eight a.m. sharp, to compare notes and start a whiteboard with what we know."

They walked quietly to the parking garage. Scott slid behind the wheel and popped open the locks so Gwen could get in on the passenger side. Scott finally let out a deep breath and said, "Captain's going to be a royal pain in the ass, Gwen. We both know that."

"It's his daughter. You can't blame him for being so upset. I think I can handle him."

"I wish you all the luck in the world. I sure hope you're right."

They drove the rest of the way across town in silence, each deep in thought.

Kathy's apartment was on the east side. It wasn't a bad neighborhood, but it was one of the older areas in town for which the city council hadn't gotten around to authorizing any revitalization projects. Huge, leaf-bare elms and maples lined cracked sidewalks, and sagging steps led to doorways with peeling paint and rotting wood.

They found a maintenance man chopping away at dead bushes with an ax on the side of the house, and after he had scrutinized the warrant carefully, he let them in.

The apartment was relatively neat and nicely furnished. A small living room was cramped with a brown leather sofa and love seat, and a stuffed chair in a blue flower fabric with a matching ottoman. A built-in bookshelf took up the far wall and was loaded with an assortment of teddy bear figurines. To the right was a tiny kitchen with a built-in counter and two barstools. Walking further into the apartment, they found that the bedroom was the largest room, taking up the entire far end of the unit. It had a walk-in closet, office area off to the right and spacious bathroom on the left.

Scott suggested, "Let's start in here, and we can let the forensics team know what to bag as we go along."

"Sure," Gwen said absentmindedly, staring in melancholy at the forest scene with black bears on the comforter covering the bed and at least a dozen stuffed bears against the headboard. Kathy saved bears of all shapes and sizes, and she smiled slightly, remembering the cuddly assortment adorning Kathy's dorm room.

"Looks like we're not the first to check out her belongings," Scott commented, jerking her out of her reverie. He had been pulling out dresser drawers.

"Why do you say that?" Gwen asked.

"Everything's been tossed. Look, every drawer is a disaster. The rest of the apartment being so neat, I doubt she'd have kept her drawers in such disarray. Look at the pile of papers pulled out of the bottom drawer." He pointed at a scattering of papers across the carpet. "Somebody was looking for something."

"Our perp?"

"Yeah, maybe. Someone she knew. He most likely had a key. It doesn't look like anyone broke in."

"Son of a bitch," Gwen muttered under her breath. "It could have been her father. He's going to be one step ahead of us this entire investigation, no doubt hiding what he doesn't want us to see. He couldn't have been very pleased with Kathy's lifestyle, and I'm certain he'll try to find her murderer before we do."

"Who would do this to Kathy?" Gwen's mind screamed with pain and frustration. Being in her apartment and touching her belongings was much harder than she'd imagined.

"No one wants their kid to be an addict. I mean, it had to be hard for him in his position to admit his daughter was a customer of the very hoodlums he was trying to lock up," Scott said wistfully.

"Well, hopefully he missed something. I'm going to the living room. I think the techs are through dusting for prints in there now. You can finish up in here."

Two hours later, they'd finished searching the apartment and found a laptop, an address book and two notebooks filled with scribbling, most of which seemed like gibberish. It was sadly the ranting and raving of a drug-crazed mind. They locked up and took the key with them since the maintenance man was nowhere to be found.

"I'm going to take the notebooks with me. Maybe I can make some sense out of them later," Gwen said wearily.

"I'll drop the laptop off on my way home. Maybe the techs can have something for us from the hard drive by morning," Scott volunteered.

"Thanks. I appreciate it."

"No problem. Goodnight."

"'Night. See you in the morning."

CHAPTER THREE

Gwen woke up bathed in sweat. She'd been dreaming about the last time she'd been with Kathy. It was the three-day weekend of Halloween, and they'd returned to Kathy's dorm in the wee hours of the morning. Hot and sweaty after parading around in her costume all day and half the night, Gwen had announced she was going to hit the showers before bed. She'd walked down the hall to the spacious bathroom shared by the occupants of the dorm's fourth floor, stripped, and stood enjoying the steady stream of hot water easing her muscles. Suddenly she realized she wasn't alone and Kathy's soapy hands had started washing her back, buttocks and legs. It had felt fabulous and she had luxuriated in the soft touch of her fingertips, never wanting her to stop.

Gwen had let it be known from her junior year of high school that she was gay, but Kathy, being the party girl and popularity queen, had never shown an interest in another woman. Feeling Kathy behind her, putting her hands on her, was a pleasant surprise she wouldn't soon forget. Gwen remembered turning and putting her hands on Kathy's breasts, kneading the firm, soft skin, and erect nipples. Their lips had met and they had hungrily taken in each other's passion.

Back in the dorm room they had made love for hours. In fact, Gwen had called police headquarters and said she'd had car trouble and couldn't make it in, which made their weekend three days instead of the planned two.

And that was it. The first and the last time she had been with Kathy. In rationalizing it, Gwen had felt that Kathy wanted to keep up appearances, and being branded a lesbian was not the image she had intended to project. Shortly afterwards Gwen heard that Kathy had married one of the popular football players from high school. Six months later, rumor had it that Kathy was already divorced. The next time Gwen heard about her was from a colleague, who had kept Kathy's name out of a sting operation from which they'd confiscated thousands of dollars in illegal drugs.

Kathy, who seemed to glide effortlessly and fit into any situation easily, was really more like an innocent and frightened animal, starved for affection. Adding to her troubled mind, Kathy found the comfort she was seeking in substances that could only cause her harm.

Gwen forced herself to remember everything Kathy had told her. Her grandmother had been an addict, and her grandfather resorted to stealing to support his wife's habit. For most of his young life, Captain Wright had grown up fatherless. His father was in and out of jail and his dazed mother mostly remained locked in her bedroom. They were poor except for the brief periods when the elder Wright found work as a plumber. Kathy's father learned at an early age how to steal to put food on the table for his family. After learning of his background Kathy told Gwen she was surprised her father joined the police force, but it was one of the few jobs available at the time that provided a decent income. She was proud of her father in that respect—he'd been able to turn his life around. Gwen surmised that it was Captain Wright's rough childhood that made him so protective of his daughter. He was strict and wanted the best for her at any cost, even when it made Kathy stubborn and rebellious.

Gwen forced herself out of bed and moved to the far end of the room to her exercise equipment. Lost in thought, she went through her hour-long exercise routine of pushups, exercise bike and weight lifting, and the time flew by. After a long hot shower, she put on thermal underwear under her gray flannel pants and donned a bulky, hunter green sweater so she would be warm enough to be able to stay outdoors as long as necessary to once more scour the crime scene.

Traffic was light at six thirty a.m. The sun was just rising and she was able to cruise easily along the county roads at a fast pace before rush hour traffic began. It took her only twenty minutes to reach the scene. Gwen parked near the point at the ravine where Kathy's car had left the road, ducked under the yellow crime scene tape, and carefully walked down to the spot they'd found Kathy's body.

There were deep ruts in the snow where the car had been towed back up the incline and taken to the police lot where it could be scoured for evidence. Gwen walked slowly in ever-widening circles and kicked at clumps of snow to make sure nothing of significance had been left behind by the techs. At the far end of the clearing, where the incline back to the road began, and where the officer had found the deep footprints, Gwen knelt and studied the route the killer would most likely have taken. He would have needed another vehicle to make his getaway, but if Kathy was already dead, how had he managed to get here with two cars? Could he have stashed a motorcycle or snowmobile? She made a note to check Kathy's car for a trailer hitch. She stood and started to walk up the slope again. Just then, she noticed someone walking twenty yards ahead, along the far side of the road. The person hadn't been visible when she had walked down the incline.

"Hey, this is a crime scene," Gwen yelled angrily. "No one's allowed in this area! Please leave immediately!"

The woman turned, a startled look on her face. "I know. I'm your new partner! They sent me out here to take a look after I checked in at the precinct." She had an identification badge around her neck over her snowsuit, the familiar yellow lanyard was blowing in the wind as she walked.

"Oh, shit," Gwen muttered under her breath as she trudged up the snowbank to catch up to the woman. "You're the newbie everyone's been whispering about?"

Gwen studied her as she waited for an answer. The woman had hair the same color as the golden retriever Gwen once had, and the way the sun reflected on the wisps of hair from the top of her head to her shoulders made her look bathed in a halo. Her eyes were deep pools of blue with little laugh lines at the edges, but now her face showed her deep concentration and was very serious.

The woman turned crimson and extended her hand, "Chloe Carpenter, but everyone calls me CC." She pulled at the jacket of her bright orange snowsuit nervously.

"Nice to meet you, CC. I'm Gwen Meyers, the detective assigned to this case. Sorry to startle you, but you know how curiosity seekers can mess up a scene. If it wasn't still so cold, there'd be plenty of onlookers trying to discover something down here and taking a bit of evidence home for their scrapbooks."

"That's okay. Officer O'Neil was supposed to let you know I was coming."

Gwen pulled out her cell phone and noticed she had a message. "Damn. I forgot to take it off vibrate, and I can't feel it over this much clothing. How long have you been out here?"

"About two hours. I wanted to scan the landscape with ultraviolet light while it was still dark to see what showed up. I didn't find any more trace, but I found a snowmobile path just on the other side of the brush across the road. It's been used recently. There are fresh skids moving away from this area, but not coming in. I found that odd," CC added, running her fingers through her long blond hair.

"So the perp must have hidden a snowmobile to get out of the area after he dumped Kathy and rolled the car! Good work."

"Thanks. Well, I guess I'm through here for now. What about you?" CC asked.

"I've got just enough time for a cup of coffee if you're interested, before I head back for the autopsy." Gwen smiled, pleased she'd been assigned a partner who wasn't afraid to dig in and work carefully and rigorously.

"Sure. That sounds great. Jackie's Deli should be open."

"Meet you there."

They arrived simultaneously at the deli and found a table in the back. Gwen ordered a ham and egg breakfast sandwich and small juice to go with her coffee, while CC opted for an English muffin and coffee.

"Any suspects?" CC asked.

"No, not yet. They haven't finished processing the car, but it looks like the perp was careful not to leave anything behind. No prints of the perp or of Kathy."

"I can tell you she wasn't ejected. She was placed in that spot on the snow," CC volunteered. "I checked the broken windows before they towed the car yesterday. No way was there enough room for a body to get through. And, though she's got plenty of bruises, there were no scratches from broken glass if she actually went through the windshield or one of the side windows. I'm waiting for my photos. I want to enlarge what I think was a fifteen-foot mark in the icy snow. I'm guessing it was made by her ring while she was being dragged."

"Wow, you are as good as they say you are!" Gwen marveled.

CC blushed again. "Just doing my job. I like it here in Scarletsville."

"Where are you from originally?" Gwen asked.

"Grew up in Milwaukee, but I attended college at the University of Wisconsin-Madison."

"That's a coincidence. That's where Kathy went."

"Oh? I didn't know that. Do you know when she graduated?"

"She didn't. She spent two years partying and then came back here. She was married a short time and worked on and off at Chuck's Garage. She got hooked on meth and coke and it really messed her up. Her dad, Captain Wright, got her into rehab, but

I don't know if she was able to stay off the stuff. Guess we'll find out at the autopsy."

CC contemplated this. "That's too bad. I didn't know what I wanted to do with my life even after I graduated from U-WM, so I went from bad jobs to worse jobs until I took a summer internship in police dispatch. I was hooked instantly and the rest is history. I've seen so many people destroy their lives one way or another. It's hard to sit back and watch. Did you know her well?"

It was Gwen's turn to blush. "Ah...yeah, pretty well a few years back. We went to high school together."

"I take it you were a couple? She was gay?" CC inquired. Then seeing the pained look on Gwen's face, she hastily added, "I'm sorry. I didn't mean to pry."

"It's okay. Nah. Nothing like that," Gwen said softly. "We'd barely started a relationship before it was over. She wasn't gay. Kathy was a free spirit. She was the type that went for the gusto. She was hell-bent on risk taking, whether it was bungee jumping or skydiving, whether or not she was scared shitless. If it was there to try, she did it. She told me about going to San Diego on a vacation. The Coast Guard had issued surf warnings, but Kathy had just learned to ride a body board. So, she ran out and caught a big wave and was dragged under. Her body was scraped and bruised from head to toe along the bottom of the ocean. She was finally dumped onto the beach by the wave, and she started laughing hysterically because she'd made it. She wasn't going to stop until she'd tried it all—and I mean tried everything and anything! I can still see the far-out look in her eyes when she told her stories—daring, relentless, and satisfied."

"I dated a woman like that for about a year. It was heartbreaking to watch her take so many stupid risks. I finally gave up trying to save her. We can't help people who aren't willing to try to save themselves. It's not your fault, Gwen."

"I know. Thank you for understanding," Gwen said, choking up.

They quit talking while the waitress put their food down and they ate in silence for a few minutes. Gwen changed the subject, they chatted about movies and books they enjoyed, and restaurants around town they both liked. When they had finished eating, CC steered the conversation back to the investigation.

"I would have liked Kathy," CC said thoughtfully. "Is her dad being a cop going to make this case more difficult for you?"

"Already has." Gwen bristled. "Scott...uh, Sergeant Richards and I searched her apartment last night. Someone had been there going through things ahead of us."

"That doesn't sound good," CC said, shaking her head. "I'll keep looking and let you know what I come up with. I thought I'd take a hike down that snowmobile trail. Now that I'm warmed up, I can head out again for a while."

"Sounds great, CC. I've got to be getting back to the precinct. Thanks for your help," Gwen said, throwing a twenty down on the table. "I'm going to enjoy working with you."

CC said confidently, "We'll make a great team. I feel it already. Hey, I'll pay for my own—" CC started to say before Gwen interrupted her.

"My treat. You can get it next time. Thanks again. See you later," Gwen said and she hurried out the door.

CHAPTER FOUR

Hmm, nice. Definitely my type, Gwen thought, driving to the station. We like the same movies and books, and the same kind of food. Yep, I definitely want to pursue this. She sure is hot, especially the dimple in her left cheek!

Arriving at the station, she parked her car on the second floor of the cement parking structure, and took the overhead walkway to the massive brick Scarletsville Police Administrative Building. She rode the elevator down to the basement morgue.

Exiting the elevator she took an immediate right and walked down the cold, granite-walled corridor, the chemical smells getting stronger every step of the way.

Dr. Berry Maynard was sitting at the reception desk talking on the phone as she entered. She waited silently as he waved and finished his conversation.

Doc was old school and ran the morgue by the book, logging everything himself and meticulously examining every inch of the bodies brought to him for autopsy. He'd once told her it wasn't that he didn't trust anyone else to help him with his work, it was just that he so enjoyed solving mysteries; he so loved exposing the evidence he retrieved from the corpses, he was reluctant to give any of it up. He had no plans to retire. A widower at sixty-four years old, he sported a long white beard but was as agile and spry as someone half his age.

"Good morning, Detective." Doc Maynard smiled at her. "A fine morning it is, but I'm afraid you missed all the excitement."

"You've already finished the autopsy?" Gwen asked anxiously.

"Not going to be one until Captain Wright's representative gets here," Doc answered grimly.

"What? How could he delay…I mean…why would he want an additional person to be present at his daughter's autopsy?" Gwen stammered.

"Doesn't want his little girl caught up in the so-called 'indignity of an autopsy'," Doc told her. "I suppose the real reason is he's going make sure I don't find anything he doesn't want found."

"This is a damn murder investigation!" Gwen replied angrily.

"Not only had his signature on the documentation, but he had the governor's approval for the delay," Doc informed Gwen.

"You know this really pisses me off," Gwen pouted, clenching her fists.

"Well, Gwen, I guess it's a good thing I did the preliminary last night," he said, a smirk on his face.

"You did? What did you find?" Gwen asked anxiously.

"I don't have all the lab work back yet, but I ordered a toxicology screening, and just on a hunch performed a pregnancy test. She was three months along."

"Phew!" Gwen exclaimed, delighted with him. "So everything isn't lost!"

"Well, I checked her skin pretty thoroughly and took pictures of the bruises. Her neck was broken at the second cervical vertebrae and petechial hemorrhages in her eyes confirmed strangulation. The bruises on both her upper arms were deep enough to indicate someone held her tightly, but I was going to measure the prints this morning. All I can say is that the hands grabbing her body were large. She had one broken fingernail on the second finger of her right hand, but again, I was waiting until this morning to get the fingernail scrapings to see if she had any of her attacker's skin lodged beneath the nails. She put up one hell of a struggle—that I could tell you for sure. Of course, lying in the snow would have cooled her body down fairly quickly, but my best estimate is that she was killed on Friday."

"So the killer kept her body for three days, then dumped her and her car out in a cow pasture! That's so weird. Doesn't make sense, does it, Doc?"

"When someone cares for the deceased, they're going to try to keep the body as long as they can. But then when decomposition begins, it takes a strong stomach to withstand the stench, or to hide it from others. I'm guessing that's the case here," Doc surmised.

"If you could have extracted the fetus, we'd have had DNA to tie-in to the father and possibly our killer, right Doc?"

"Absolutely," he agreed.

"Do you have any idea when this 'representative' of the captain is supposed to get here?" Gwen asked.

"Can't tell you that," Doc said, scratching his chin through his thick beard. "I plan on sleeping on the cot in my office. Could be anytime after midnight."

"I'll leave my cell phone on. You'll call me if you discover anything new?"

"Sure will, Detective. This little girl didn't deserve what she got. I'll be thorough no matter who's watching me work."

***

Gwen slept fitfully on and off, and at six a.m. she gave up, threw on her robe, padded into her kitchen in her bare feet, and flipped the switch to start a pot of coffee. When it was done, she paced until she couldn't stand it anymore. At seven a.m. she called Doctor Maynard. Doc picked up on the first ring.

"Were you able to autopsy Kathy?" Gwen blurted out.

"Yep. We finished about two a.m. I didn't want to call and wake you. Besides, I won't know any more until I receive the lab results," Doc said kindly.

"Who was the surprise representative?" Gwen asked curiously.

"Oh, just some fancy, highfalutin' doctor from Madison. Thought he knew more than I did, but I put him in his place right quick. Don't worry, I got all I needed."

"Where is she now—still in the morgue?"

"Nope. They whisked her out of here as soon as the autopsy was finished. That damn funeral home hurried me through the paperwork like there was no tomorrow," Doc harrumphed.

"I'd better get over to the funeral home. Mac Tranard has the body?"

"Yep, picked her up at five a.m. sharp."

"Thanks, Doc. Call me when you get the toxicology results, please?"

"Sure will, Detective. You take care now."

Gwen raced to her car and hurried to the Tranard Funeral Home.

As she was pulling into the parking lot, Mac was exiting through the back door. Gwen jumped out and approached the thin, middle-aged man. Mac had inherited the family business about two years ago. With his irritating, high-pitched, squeaky voice, and gruff manner, she was surprised he was still making a go of it.

"I understand you have the Wright body. I'd like to see it," Gwen barked as she approached him.

"Kinda late for that. She's been in the crematorium for... uh..." Looking at his expensive-looking gold watch, Mac continued with a smug look on his face, "Two hours and twenty-three minutes."

"What was the rush, Mac?" she asked urgently.

"Dunno. It's what Captain Wright wanted. He wants services ASAP. Gotta please the customers, ya know, Detective Meyers, whether they be dead or alive," he said sarcastically.

"Guess it's time to get some answers from Captain Wright myself," Gwen muttered as she stomped back to her car.

CHAPTER FIVE

Arriving at the North Precinct, Gwen didn't bother stopping to announce herself. She found Captain Wright in his office and she barged in, letting the door close behind her with a loud bang.

"Detective Meyers! Happy to see you! I hope you're here with the good news that you've arrested my daughter's killer," Wright said gruffly.

He stood behind a battered wooden desk, which was empty save for one thin file folder. Behind him were shelves filled with baseball trophies from the precinct teams he'd coached. On each side of the bookshelf were gold-framed pictures of the captain standing with various dignitaries, most of whom Gwen didn't recognize, the pictures were so old.

"Captain Wright, I just found out you had Kathy's body cremated already. If I didn't know better, I would think you were trying to hide evidence."

"Now Gwen," he said calmly, sitting down in an expensive black leather chair which looked out of place behind the battered desk. "I remember you coming to the house frequently when you and my daughter were in high school. You were almost like a second daughter to me back then, and now look at you. You've made detective, and from what I hear, a damn good one. You don't mind if I still call you Gwen, do you?"

He didn't wait for an answer before continuing, "You and I have both spent more time than we'd like to remember in the morgue. Kathy wasn't some common slut or whore picked up off the streets. I couldn't bear the thought of her lying on a cold slab in that place for one more minute. Can't you understand that? Just think if it had been your own flesh and blood. Your job is to conduct this investigation, and mine is to bury my daughter properly," he said, his eyes tearing up.

"You're not helping me catch her killer," Gwen said, standing her ground. "If anything, you're impeding the investigation."

"By the way, you know I am aware of the relationship you had with my daughter," Wright snapped back. "I could have you taken off this case. Can you understand that?"

"You know that no one would work this case as hard as I will to find her murderer," Gwen said crisply.

"I know. That's why I haven't said anything. But be assured, Detective Meyers, if you cross the line with me, I will have you off this case, pronto. And, I'll make sure you're demoted to patrol."

"Yes, I'm sure you would do that," Gwen said angrily. "Just one question. Did you know she was pregnant?"

The rapid flush of his face and startled expression told her he'd had no idea. "No. That's not true," he said, stunned.

"Doc Maynard ran the test last night. It's true," Gwen divulged. "Do you know who she was dating? Any idea who the father could be?"

Wright slumped back into his chair with a defeated sigh. "She was in with a bad crowd. I tried everything I could to get her back on track and off the drugs. I'd hoped after she got out of rehab she could change her life around. But she kept sneaking around with those assholes down on Main Street. They're the ones that got her hooked. I don't have any names, but I can pull the arrest warrants for anyone we nabbed over the past year. Maybe that would help give you some leads."

"I'd appreciate that, Captain," Gwen replied tersely.

She turned and walked briskly out of his office.

"He is and always was a Class A jerk," Gwen muttered to herself as she strode to her car. "He gives real meaning to the term 'bad cop/good cop.'" She could easily imagine him in the role of badgering a suspect into giving a false confession just to get him out of their face. Kathy had never had anything good to say about her father, and Gwen could now see why. She swallowed the lump in her throat remembering all the conversations she'd had with Kathy. They'd told each other everything about their childhoods, and Kathy's had not been pleasant with her overbearing and verbally abusive father.

Gwen had time to make one more stop before she made it back to her precinct to meet with her staff and get their updates. The sun was shining brightly and the streets were wet, absorbing the runoff of melting snow. Gwen guessed it must be close to forty degrees, and she decided to slip into the ladies' room to shed her long underwear before going back to her car.

***

She'd known Eric Kaplan since she was a kid. His parents were hard-working farmers, and Eric had missed a lot of school when his help was needed on the family farm. She would miss him when he wasn't on the school bus taking them to Scarletsville Elementary. He was bigger than the other boys his age and most of the kids a year or two older, and no one teased her about her tomboy appearance when he was around. His mother had passed away the previous spring, but Eric still worked hard and took excellent care of his father and the farm. His older siblings had all moved on to bigger cities and jobs that were more glamorous. His father had to be in his early sixties by now. He was the "ol' man

Kaplan" the officer had mentioned, who had called 911 after he'd heard Kathy's car crash into his pastureland.

The Kaplan farm was well kept on a sprawling fifty-acre plot. Eric, like his father, kept the land primarily for dairy farming, but he also fattened a good number of cattle for slaughter. The Kaplans were well known for their fresh eggs sold for "a buck a dozen" and the chicken coop was always filled with several dozen golden brown and white hens. Gwen supposed Eric also used a large portion of his land for growing ginseng. More than one farmer in this area had quickly become a millionaire after the plant became a popular medicinal herb and vitamin supplement.

Gwen found Eric in his barn under a tractor, repairing the blade apparatus.

"Just in time," Eric called out when he saw her. "Can you hold this wrench while I tighten the bolt?"

Gwen chuckled. "Sure thing. I'd be glad to help."

When Eric finished, he wiped his hands on a dirty rag hanging out of his baggy overalls and thanked her with a crooked grin on his face. "I don't imagine you came all the way out here to help me," he said.

Gwen noticed that the twenty-six-year-old man had gained several pounds since she last saw him. With jet-black hair starting to prematurely gray at the temples and long disheveled locks touching below his collar, he was still as handsome as ever.

"I just wanted to find out if you had heard anything else last night around the time of the crash. I heard your father was the one who called nine-one-one."

"You know, I heard a motor sputtering just after my dad called it in. I thought it was weird that someone was out that late on a snowmobile. But there's a lot of them in this area at all times of the day and night, so I didn't think anything more about it. She lost control is what I heard one of the cops say."

"She was murdered, Eric. The body was already dead when it landed in your pasture."

"My God, I didn't even think of that. Well then, I guess it could have been a snowmobile I heard shortly after the crash after all." Eric rubbed his eyes with the cleanest corner of his oily rag, clearly horrified at the thought of the dead body lying on his property. "I swear, I'd have run out to the field immediately had I thought anyone had been hurt. God, I feel awful about this."

"Did you see anyone or hear anything else?" Gwen prodded.

"The crash is what woke me up. I yelled to Dad to call in the emergency. I grabbed a jacket and ran to the edge of the fence. I was just standing there when the snowmobile came to life, but the path is on the other side of the road, way out of my view," Eric told her. "The car crash was what we were concentrating on. It was a tremendous noise, creaking and bending metal—it had to be loud for Dad to hear it. He's gotten considerably hard of hearing over the years." He grinned. "Sometimes I think it's just him being obstinate, preferring not to listen to half of what I say."

Gwen chuckled. "Okay, well, thanks for your help, Eric. It was nice seeing you again."

"You too, Gwen. Stop by anytime. I've got plenty of work if you decide to change careers," he said and laughed.

"I'll remember that," Gwen said. She was still chuckling at the thought as she got into her car.

CHAPTER SIX

The rest of her team was already assembled when Gwen arrived at the police station. Jenny was writing on a big whiteboard in the messy squad room, listing the known facts of the murder on the top, and adding more to the board as the other team members gave the results of their inquiries during the past twenty-four hours. Scott was briefing them on the results of Kathy's car as Gwen walked in. There were photos, papers, files and empty food wrappers everywhere. There was a tape player sitting in the middle of a long conference table taking up most of the space in the room, so they could replay recordings of the interviews repeatedly to listen for any additional clues. Next to the tape recorder was the morning newspaper. They'd made the front page, with an old photograph of Kathy as a teenager in a cheerleading outfit staring back at them. Next to her was a recent picture of the captain.

"We found a match to the prints left in the snow on the driver's side of the vehicle. Same boot pattern and size. Problem is, so many outlets carry them, we'll never be able to tie anyone in by the impression," Scott disclosed. "Except there's one small fissure made in the snow. So far, I don't know if it was a leaf or twig on the surface or a crack in the boot. If it's the boots, they'd be good evidence. That is if we can find them."

"I have three contacts who knew Kathy from the streets," Jenny told the team. "I've talked with the first two and I'll meet with the third tonight. The first said she hadn't seen Kathy in two or three months. She told me she had heard Kathy had gone into rehab and cleaned up her act. The second, a young man, knew her better and confirmed that Kathy had stopped using. He mentioned she went into rehab and quit cold turkey. That was right after she'd found out that she was pregnant. He didn't know who the father was."

"Put that on the board, Jenny," Gwen added. "Doc Maynard confirmed she was three months pregnant."

"That fits," Brad remarked. "I checked with Holy Cross Rehabilitation Center. She was admitted for a two-week stay and was released a week ago. That means she'd been clean a little more than three weeks. I have an appointment to review her records with the administrator tomorrow."

"Doc was sharp enough to do the blood work last night, so we'll soon have the confirmation to prove she was pregnant," Gwen added. She then proceeded to tell the group about Captain Wright delaying the autopsy until he could get a physician from Madison to assist.

Jenny piped in, "My source put me onto this third individual. I'm sorry, but they've all got criminal records, so I promised not to reveal any of their names in this investigation. The young man feels this third person knew Kathy well enough to know who the father was. They shared a flophouse near Main Street when they were using. I'm meeting her at a coffeehouse later, right down the street from their residence."

"Sure you don't need backup?" Scott asked seriously, staring at her with his intense blue eyes and absentmindedly wrapping his fingers around the end of his ponytail.

Jenny grinned. "No, they're mixed-up kids, but not violent." She patted her Glock. "I don't think I need to worry."

"Any other friends?" Gwen asked, looking at Scott.

"I've checked out about half the names so far from the address book we found in Kathy's apartment. Most haven't been in touch with her for months, if not years. I left a message for a Jerry Kingley. Someone suggested he may have been dating her, but he hasn't returned my call yet. I'll hunt him down later if I don't hear something soon."

"Oh," Brad interjected. "The hard drive on her laptop was wiped clean, but we think we can still retrieve some of the files. The lab guys are still working on it." He stroked his mustache and winked knowingly, assuring them he could salvage some possibly valuable information.

Just then, "The Star-Spangled Banner" started playing and Scott stifled a huge grin as he pulled his cell phone out of his pocket.

"Yeah, Jerry, thanks for returning my call," Scott said. "I'm Sergeant Richards of the Scarletsville PD, and we're investigating the death of Kathy Wright." Scott was silent for a few seconds before he spoke again. "Sorry you had to hear about it that way, buddy. How about I buy you a beer over on Twenty-Fourth and Nash, say in an hour? Great. Thanks."

When he'd signed off on the call, Scott told the group, "He got a call from Captain Wright ripping him a new you-know-what for getting his daughter pregnant and then blaming Jerry that she was dead."

"We've got so little to go on as it is, I wish Wright would keep his nose out of it!" Gwen said angrily. "He wasn't aware his daughter was pregnant. That was clear from my visit with him. But he also said he didn't know any of her boyfriends. I'll throw that back in his face when we have our next 'discussion.' Brad, if you don't mind, see if you can put the heat on someone at the North Precinct. Captain Wright seemed to think there might be a connection between his daughter's death and recent drug arrests. We need names and addresses. Then have one of the uniforms visit these folks and check their alibis. Bring in anyone that doesn't have one. Anyone have anything else?"

When no one responded, Gwen told them they'd meet again the next day and she dismissed them. She rushed out of the conference room and nearly collided in the hallway with CC.

CC laughed at the surprised look on Gwen's face. "I was hoping I'd find you here. Do you have a few minutes?"

"Uh, sure. I'll fill you in on the task force meeting while we eat. Can we get out of here and grab a hamburger or something? I haven't eaten since breakfast," Gwen said, rubbing her stomach.

"You just reminded me, neither have I. That sounds terrific. Let's go!"

The Main Street Pub was an old greasy spoon crammed with a dozen tables around the perimeter and one long table in the center for larger groups, but the food was cheap and plentiful and it was located directly across from the station, so it was a favorite cop hangout.

When they were seated at one of the small tables toward the back of the pub waiting for their hamburger and fries, CC revealed what she had come up with. Gwen could tell she was excited, and had to lean forward so none of the other patrons could hear their whispered conversation. "The streak across the ice definitely came from Kathy's ring. Therefore, she was dragged at least fifteen feet. Someone probably carried her down the incline and dropped her, then decided to move her farther away, not knowing exactly where the car would end up when it was pushed over the side. I also followed the snowmobile path, and listen to this. It may not be from our perp, but you never know." CC told her about calling for a lab tech to come back to collect a square of blue denim fabric about an inch long. "There were discarded Coke bottles and coffee cups, but they were all too old to have been tossed recently. The lab guy insisted on bagging a few anyway."

Gwen beamed. "The fabric is a great find. Now all we have to do is find the jacket or jeans with the missing swatch. It's like a mosaic, CC. As each piece is filled in, we'll have a complete picture of our perp. It's not much so far, but I really believe we can catch this creep," Gwen said confidently.

"I believe we will too," CC said as their food was delivered. "Umm, these burgers look yummy!"

Their conversation drifted back to their personal lives as they ate. CC told of her life in Milwaukee, being the youngest of seven children—she had four brothers and two sisters. She was loved and doted on by all her siblings and parents. They were a close-knit family and had spent much of every summer camping, fishing and boating in the north woods where they owned a lake cottage. Her dad was a retired high school principal and her mother owned a small jewelry store and repair business, which her sisters were in the process of taking over so her mom could enjoy retirement with her dad.

Gwen listened with envy, revealing she had only one brother, who was killed in a tragic accident in the army two years ago. A bunch of the guys in his troop had been moving ammo out of a warehouse when it exploded. They thought someone tossed a lit cigarette to scare the others, thinking there would be only a small explosion, but there wasn't much evidence left to confirm that premise or to convict any of the few survivors. Her brother had been seven years older, so she might as well have been an only child. The two of them never were close and had fought constantly when they were together. Her dad had been an executive for Sea-Cal, the giant petroleum company, but had died of a massive heart attack when she was fifteen. Her mother was now suffering from multiple sclerosis and spending the rest of her days in Pineview, a nursing home on the shore of Lake Powder.

"A lot of tragedy in your family," commented CC. "I'm sorry you had to go through all of that."

Gwen only nodded sadly, and they sat in silence for a few minutes while they ate. Gwen hated like hell that she still hurt so badly inside when she talked about her family, and couldn't stand the look of pity on CC's face.

When Gwen finally looked up from her plate, CC was staring at a table of noisy patrons and not at her any longer, so she launched into filling CC in on all that had transpired at the task force meeting. The pain of Gwen's past quickly dissipated as the two women discussed the case.

As she was picking through the remnants of the pile of onion rings and fries they'd shared, Gwen's cell phone rang.

"Detective Meyers," she said curtly.

"Gwen, you'd better get over here," Jenny said nervously. "I got a call from my last contact, Cyndi Jeffries. She asked me to hurry. She was frightened. I'm at the flophouse now where she lived. She'd asked me to meet her down the street for a cup of coffee, but when she didn't show, I came to the address my other contact had given me. She's dead."

"On my way," Gwen said quickly, getting the location and signing off.

She filled CC in on the latest development and signaled for their check.

"I'd like to come along if you don't mind," CC said.

Gwen winked and smiled. "I found out this morning, you're officially on the task force and as my new partner, you'll be sticking with me closely. Maybe we can get some good trace this time before the animals start tromping the scene to bits! Welcome aboard!"

CHAPTER SEVEN

The flophouse was in one of the poorest sections of Scarletsville, not far from Main Street where the hookers, drug addicts and pimps made their living. Three quarters of the buildings had been boarded up for years, but that didn't stop those who were down on their luck or spaced out on drugs from making them their own. Rusted out vehicles and garbage adorned many of the front yards, sagging porches drooped precariously, and peeling paint rippled on the cheaply made wooden structures. The stench of backed-up sewers assaulted their senses as they screeched to a halt in front of the address Jenny had given them.

They had to be careful walking the cracked sidewalk, choked with tangled, out of control weeds. Someone had shoveled the width of a ten-inch shovel blade, but left patches of ice that could easily throw someone sprawling onto their rear.

"I'm so glad you're here!" Jenny announced, opening the door as soon as they got up to the porch.

"What time did you get here?" Gwen asked, pulling out her notebook.

"Fifteen-fifty-eight. Uh, about twenty minutes ago," Jenny answered. "The screen door was unlocked, the inner door wide open. I walked only as far as the living room calling for Cyndi. I checked for a pulse, and when I couldn't find one, I called you. I've been waiting at the door so I wouldn't contaminate anything."

"Good girl," Gwen complimented her.

"Uh, if you don't need me, I've got paperwork to catch up on back at the station."

She looked greenish. Finding a dead body was not an easy matter even for veteran cops.

"Sure," Gwen said kindly. "And thanks. You handled this very well."

"Thanks," Jenny said, hurrying out the door, just as the coroner's assistant and evidence tech entered. Gwen had called them on the way over.

The coroner's assistant was already inching forward, gazing intently at the floor as she walked, and was pulling tweezers and evidence bags out of her backpack simultaneously. She and the evidence tech had bagged three mysterious items by the time they reached the body.

"Hello, Doctor Lindsey," Gwen greeted her. She had worked with this woman a few times before. The short, heavyset Lindsey looked like the grandmotherly type with close-cropped steel hair and a double chin, but she was anything but pleasant. She grunted in return and kept working. The tall, Hispanic, gangly evidence tech was unfamiliar. After introducing himself as Javier, he raised his eyebrows and followed his boss.

Cyndi was an emaciated black female with beautiful, unblemished cocoa-colored skin. Her smudged makeup had been applied generously—dark red lip gloss, thick black eyeliner. An unnatural red blush with tiny sparkles glistened on her cheeks. Long, manicured nails were painted the same deep red as her lips. Her glossy black hair was braided into tight dreadlocks, with copper-colored beads woven into the knots of hair. Purple and green bruising was starting to deepen in color around her neck and a small trickle of blood oozed from the back of her head. Lindsey had the tech take several pictures before carefully turning Cyndi's head. Gwen saw that she had a triangular wound at the top of her skull where the hair had been ripped away, possibly caused by hitting her head on the wooden crate in front of the ripped, green vinyl sofa.

The room's furnishings were what Gwen liked to refer to as "junkyard style"—old, worn and battered. A wooden desk in the corner was deeply scarred and the bottom shelf of a four-shelf bookcase had a hole in it large enough to put her arm through. There were no pictures on the walls or any knickknacks, which would have lent a personal touch to the surroundings. A dirty, lime-green overstuffed chair had lost much of its padding and tilted to the right with one of its wooden legs missing. The dull brown parquet wooden floor was partially covered with a dirty area rug with a paisley pattern in green, brown, red and black.

Cyndi was wearing a long-sleeved, oversized denim shirt over a pair of red bikini underpants. Her legs and feet were bare. It was hardly dress one would wear to answer the door to greet guests. She had to have been surprised by her attacker while getting ready to meet with Jenny at the diner down the street, unless she was familiar enough with her attacker to have let him in half clothed.

"I always find it hard to imagine that people actually live in these kinds of surroundings," CC said grimly. "This place is filthy."

"It's like this and much worse when they're desperate, especially when they're hooked on drugs," Gwen replied. "It's hard to imagine Kathy staying in this place. I mean, she always seemed like such a clean freak."

"I guess you're right. The drugs give you a whole new perspective on things and what's important to you," CC agreed.

"I'm going to vacuum her shirt and the carpet around her," Javier said, letting them know they were in his way.

Javier pulled a tiny, battery-powered vacuum from his

backpack and carefully covered every inch of the shirt's front. Doctor Lindsey helped hold the body at an angle so he could access her back. Javier then skillfully placed the filter into a plastic evidence cylinder, labeled it for the lab, and repeated the process with the surrounding carpet.

While they were finishing their examination, Gwen got up to check out the rest of the house. The walls leading to the bedroom were a dirty yellow, streaked brown in places where the roof had leaked rain and melting snow. The only items in the tiny bedroom were two single mattresses on the floor with rumpled gray sheets and blankets, and three cardboard boxes filled with clothes. There was a small bathroom with sink, shower, and commode to the right of the bedroom. It was the only room that looked like anyone had attempted to clean, except for rust stains embedded deeply into the yellow, faded porcelain surfaces. The counter next to the sink was stacked with an assortment of makeup in every brand and color—lipsticks, blush, foundation, eyeliner with matching eye shadow, nail polish, facial creams. On the floor in the shower were several brands of shampoo, hair rinse and scented soaps.

Gwen opened the wooden cabinet next to the sink. Under a stack of towels was a shoebox filled with drug paraphernalia—pipes, rolling papers, needles and syringes. A plastic baggie contained only a thin film of white powder. She left the box on the counter, and made a note to have the techs test the baggie for what she was certain was cocaine.

When she returned to the living room, Gwen found Javier and CC examining with a magnifying glass a locket embedded in the folds of the dead girl's neck. It was a gold necklace with a heart-shaped charm about the size of a dime.

Javier looked up and said, "The doctor had to leave, so I'll continue gathering evidence. She said she'd e-mail her report."

"Okay," Gwen sighed, wishing she had been able to talk with the doctor before she'd left so quickly.

"Do you know Kathy's birth date?" CC asked softly.

"Uh, late October. I remember in school we teased her about being born so close to Halloween."

"There's a beautiful opal mounted on the front. That would be the right birthstone, and the name Kathy is inscribed on the back."

"My God, she's wearing Kathy's necklace?" Gwen asked, momentarily dazed.

"Looks like it."

Gwen remembered Kathy's smooth, creamy skin and suckling at her earlobes, running her tongue down her neck. Kathy had never taken that necklace off. The sturdy but delicate metal links were 24-carat gold and the opal a perfect oval. When they'd taken a break from their lovemaking and finished eating bagels with cream cheese and orange marmalade in bed, Gwen had stuck her finger in the sweet and sticky jelly and swirled it around Kathy's breasts, licking them clean afterward. Kathy had jokingly scolded her for soiling her precious pendant.

"Gwen, are you okay?" CC asked, breaking her reverie.

"Oh, ah…yeah. Sorry. It does look like the one Kathy always wore. Find anything else?"

"I have two short hairs I discovered stuck to the sole of her right foot. They look silver gray in this light, but they could be eyelashes powdered with her makeup. Doesn't look like there are roots, so I doubt we'll be able to get DNA, but we should be able to confirm pretty easily whether or not they're Cyndi's or someone else's," Javier volunteered.

"Well, at least that's something. At least we have something to go on. Do you need more time?" Gwen smiled.

"You two can leave if you'd like. I'm used to working alone," Javier said brusquely. "Besides, I'm sure the doc will be sending me some help. We can't be too careful."

"Take as long as you want. Here's my cell number if you find anything I should know about immediately," Gwen said before she and CC headed out the door.

CHAPTER EIGHT

It was nearly eight p.m. and time to meet the rest of the team at headquarters before they finished interviewing neighbors, returned to talk with Javier and the rest of the team that had assembled, and wrapped it up at the crime scene. The coroner confirmed by e-mail that Cyndi had been dead for only minutes before Jenny had found her. She had, perhaps, even scared the perpetrator away when she arrived. A small window in the bedroom had been left open, and would have been an easy route out of the apartment for the killer. The alley behind the house would have allowed him to escape unnoticed by anyone from the street.

When they entered the squad room, they saw Jenny sitting quietly by herself toward the back of the room. She was writing in a small notebook. She was still pale, but looked more serene, having lost the "deer caught in the headlights" gaze she'd displayed at the crime scene.

CC and Gwen came up to her and Gwen said cheerfully, "Hey, kiddo. How are you doing?"

Startled and obviously still jumpy, she said, "Oh, hi. Okay, I guess."

"Don't be so hard on yourself," CC whispered. "You'll get used to it."

"Yeah, it's difficult even for us, and we've been first on the scene dozens of times," Gwen confided.

"Really?" Jenny asked, her eyes wide.

"Really," both CC and Gwen said in unison. The three women started laughing, easing the tension, just as Scott and Brad walked in.

"We could use some of that humor," Brad said with a smile. "What's so funny?"

"Sorry, Brad," Gwen replied. "It's a woman thing. You guys wouldn't understand."

"Try us," Scott said kiddingly, poking Gwen in the arm lightly with his fist.

"In your dreams," Gwen shot back. "Okay guys, what do you have for us?"

CC reddened, as if remembering something she had forgotten to tell Gwen about. "Geez, I almost forgot. I found a cell phone under the couch when Javier was working on Cyndi. He bagged it and put it in the evidence locker."

"Great find!" Gwen exclaimed. "Brad, can you get the lab on it ASAP when we're through here?" She ran to the whiteboard to add it to the list of evidence, starting a new column for information regarding Cyndi. In a broad stroke, she drew an arrow from Cyndi's name to Kathy's.

"You got it," he said, pulling out his notebook.

"Talked to the boyfriend, Jerry Kingley," Scott told them. "Definitely not our guy for the murder, but he could be the father of Kathy's unborn child. He admitted they'd been intimate for the past year. He's worried sick about the father. Says Kathy always said her father was nuts, though he'd never met the guy and has no idea who told the captain he'd been dating his daughter. They'd kept it secret just for that reason. Seems the captain liked to break up any serious relationships Kathy had. He hadn't seen Kathy for the past week because he was in Illinois with the National Guard. I confirmed he was out of town when Kathy was killed. No way he could have done it even with an overnight pass. Several witnesses were with him in a Guard meeting until nine p.m. and they were up at dawn for war games which lasted all the following day."

"I have a hard time picturing a member of the National Guard with a druggie," Brad said, shaking his head.

"He was gone a lot," Scott continued, standing up as he talked. He waved his arms in the air as he talked, emphasizing his remarks. "He always let her know in advance, though, when he'd be on furlough. Jerry said she was more a recreational user, didn't use much when he was around unless they were at a party and others were passing stuff around. He said it wasn't a problem in their relationship. She told him she could quit anytime. He was surprised when she entered rehab, since he just didn't think she was a hard-core user."

"But they did have a permanent relationship?" Gwen asked. "Or were they off and on again? I can't picture Kathy with someone like him either."

"It was permanent for the little time he was in town. He said she was beautiful, charming, funny. They enjoyed the same things and cherished the little time they could spend together. I found Kingley to be a nice guy. He was realistic though, saying they hadn't made long-term plans because neither knew when they'd be ready to settle down. He was shocked to hear she was pregnant. Looks like she kept that from him too. Now that she's gone, he said there was nothing to keep him in Scarletsville, especially with the captain gunning for him. He plans to move closer to the base in Illinois." Scott gave them a confident look and sat back down, straddling the chair backward and folding his arms against his chest.

"You don't think he's running?" CC asked, still doubtful.

"No, not at all. He returned my call as soon as he was able and gave me a couple other numbers where I could reach him on base. No, I'd stake my reputation on him not having anything to do with her murder."

"That's good enough for me," Gwen announced, leaving the whiteboard and moving closer to where the group sat. "Anyone else have anything?"

"They found a half dozen short silver hairs in Kathy's vehicle. They're in the lab now for testing," Brad offered.

"I'd like to compare them with the ones found on Cyndi," CC said thoughtfully.

"Sure. If you can give me what you have, I can get Charlie right on it. That's it for the car—we swept it thoroughly, but someone had wiped it clean before leaving it in Kaplan's field. It's ready for the junkyard," Brad admitted, his sharp tone indicating his frustration.

"By any chance did you notice whether there was a trailer hitch for a snowmobile on the back?" Gwen asked evenly.

"Fairly certain there wasn't, but I'll double-check on that," Brad said, writing a reminder in his notebook.

"I still have about a dozen names to contact from her address book," Scott announced. "By the way, Gwen, you find anything in those notebooks of Kathy's?"

"Haven't had a chance for more than a quick look. They're still sitting in my den at home. I promise to look through them more thoroughly tonight. Thanks for reminding me."

"I'd like to take a look when you're done," Scott told her. "I'm still trying to figure out how some of the names I've come across fit into her lifestyle. Maybe the journals will give me some clues."

"No problem. You'll have them tomorrow. We should have the tech reports on Cyndi Jeffries first thing in the morning. I'd like you to compare them with Kathy Wright's, Brad," Gwen instructed him, walking to the whiteboard again. "Jenny, if you have time maybe you can help Scott track down the contacts in Kathy's phone book, and CC, I sure could use your help locating anyone who knew Cyndi."

"I'd be happy to help, partner." CC smiled. She got up and walked to where Gwen was standing. Gwen knew they both wished there was more they could add to the evidence columns.

"Great. Now that we have two murders, we sure can use more help," Gwen remarked.

Brad stood and stretched, then said, "As long as you're begging for more help, we could use someone in Narcotics who's familiar with the Main Street area. I know you two women are capable, but it might be safer to assign one of the men to help get information from the crazies down there."

"Point well taken," Gwen said. "We can find out if Vice has any informants who may be willing to divulge information. Our perp had to have been in the area quite a few times. I would think he'd have watched the women for some time to know their schedules and determine the best time to nab them. He grabbed Kathy, willingly or not, and entered the flophouse in plain daylight to kill Cyndi. Someone had to see something. You're right. Someone in Narcotics could prove very helpful. Anything else?"

When no one spoke up, Gwen continued, "First thing tomorrow morning I'm going to pay another visit to Captain Wright. Let's find out what he has to say about Cyndi's murder. And why he lied to me about Kathy's boyfriend. See you all tomorrow."

CHAPTER NINE

Gwen took a long hot bath when she got home and settled into her bed wearing her flannel pajamas. With a cup of hot tea on her nightstand, she started reading the two notebooks she'd taken from Kathy's apartment. It was painful to know she was reading the diaries of a woman she had once loved who was now dead.

Trying to get some timeframe as to when they were written, Gwen noticed tiny lettering on the bottom of every ninth or tenth page showing the date. The second notebook was only half filled, so she started with that one, reading the most recent entries first and going backward in time.

On the day before her murder, she had been struggling with telling Jerry about the pregnancy. If she decided to abort, she wouldn't have to tell him at all. She liked the idea of entering into motherhood, but knew she could not afford to support the baby on her limited income.

Kathy wrote several pages about how furious her father would be when he discovered her pregnancy. Surely there would be no more handouts of twenty-dollar bills when she begged for money, and the occasional dinner she was treated to when his mood was hospitable. His reaction would certainly be one reason to opt for abortion.

Keeping the baby meant visiting an obstetrician regularly and starting on a regimen of vitamins and calcium. There was no way she could do that without Jerry's financial support. She'd learned she was expecting from the results of cheap, drugstore urine tests. She wondered if they could be giving her false readings, even though she'd tested herself three times, on three consecutive days. Thus far, she'd only had minimal nausea in the morning, and nothing like the violent morning sickness she'd heard others talk about. The thought of drinking milk made her want to vomit. She missed her vodka tonics, but needed to be strong and stick to her program, regardless of the pregnancy.

She wrote pages and pages about what a nice guy Jerry was and how much she enjoyed being with him. She wasn't in love but wondered, given the right circumstances, if she could fall in love and be with him "till death do us part." He was great in bed, and liked the same music, TV programs and movies as she did. Never before had she dated someone so "squeaky-clean." In her journals were notes on every date they'd had in the past year—movies, parties, long walks, in-depth conversations about life and what their fondest hopes and dreams were. She admitted he was more than a brotherly figure, but less than her knight in shining armor. Maybe, she had pondered, there wasn't such a thing, at least not for her.

Many of the writings were assignments from her stay in rehabilitation. She wrote daily about how great she felt and how staying off the drugs had opened her eyes to the value of a clean and sober life. Every day she vowed to make it through whatever she came up against without getting high. She needed to find a Narcotics Anonymous meeting soon, as she had promised to do upon release from her inpatient stay. She already had a sponsor who, she wrote in her journal, was "keeping her strong." She called Lisa every day, whether she was feeling up or down, and Lisa was the only one she had confided in about her pregnancy. Gwen made a note to try to find "Lisa," but knowing the anonymity of the program, that was sure to prove difficult.

Gwen felt guilty reading some of the entries she was sure Kathy would never have divulged to anyone, least of all a former lover like herself. And the more she read, the more Gwen realized she hadn't known Kathy at all. During their night of lovemaking, Kathy had asked a million questions of Gwen; she had asked about all her former lovers, what she liked and didn't like about her life, and about things that had happened as she was growing up. She had wanted to know how Gwen had reacted and how it had affected her life afterward. Kathy had revealed little about herself. She was wrapped up in a cocoon of her own emotions and trying to learn how to act by following the direction of those people she admired. Had Gwen not been so stupid, had she seen the signs of depression she'd studied since joining the police force, perhaps she would have been able to make a difference in Kathy's life and things would have turned out differently. Gwen berated herself for not keeping in touch. She wiped the tears from her eyes and returned to the notebooks. Most of the earliest writings were gibberish that Gwen couldn't decipher. Clearly, she had been high when she had started keeping her logs.

At six a.m. Gwen awoke to the annoying buzzing sound of her alarm clock. Hopefully she could get into the office before the others and check her e-mails to see if the lab had found anything new. She'd fallen asleep reading Kathy's journals. Groaning, she reached over to turn off the alarm and woke up fully while she was going through her exercise routine. She tried to put Kathy out of her mind as she showered, made a cup of instant coffee and sat at her kitchen nook to read the paper.

The accident was front page news again. The headline read, "Police Captain's Daughter Dead in Crash."

"So they haven't figured out yet that the police are conducting a murder investigation," Gwen mused.

The article reported that the car sliding off the highway due to the slippery roads had caused the tragic accident. Perfect to keep the press out of their hair, hopefully for a few days or until they could catch the creep who'd put Kathy there.

After skimming through the rest of the paper, Gwen grabbed her coat and headed out the door. Just as she slid into her car, her cell phone rang.

"Gwen, I have the results of the tox screenings," Doc Maynard told her. "No illegal drugs in her body, but a heap of over-the-counter vitamins."

"Glad to hear that," Gwen replied.

"Doesn't help you much, but it will be comforting to the family to know she was clean as a whistle."

"Yes, Doc, I'm sure her father will be pleased," Gwen said, smiling.

Her cell rang again.

"Hi, Gwen. It's CC. Hope I didn't wake you."

"No," Gwen laughed. "I don't have time for the luxury of sleeping in today. I'm on my way to the North Precinct to see Captain Wright now. What's up?"

"The cell phone I found under the couch wasn't Cyndi's. It belonged to Kathy. We're getting a printout of all calls in and out from her carrier. We should have the information this afternoon."

"Hmm…good news. It ties Kathy with Cyndi, and proves Kathy had been to the flophouse. Odd she'd leave without her cell phone, but maybe she didn't know she'd lost it."

"That's what I thought, unless Cyndi had some reason to steal it from Kathy's purse, then slip it under the couch to hide it."

"We'll probably never know, but at least we'll know who Kathy was in contact with on the days leading up to her death," Gwen said thoughtfully.

"Yeah. Good luck with Captain Grouch," CC teased.

"Thanks," Gwen laughed. "I'll give you a call when I'm done. I'd like to hit the downtown area afterward if you're up to it."

"That's a plan. I'll be waiting in the lab, comparing notes from both scenes."

CHAPTER TEN

Captain Wright wasn't in his office when Gwen arrived, but he bustled in shortly after she had him paged. He had an expectant look on his face. His uniform looked rumpled, unlike the starched appearance she'd noticed during her last visit.

"I hope you're here to tell me the good news that you've arrested my daughter's killer," he said anxiously.

"No sir. We're working every angle," Gwen added.

"That Jerry King...Kingston...or, Kingley, that's it. You've not arrested him?" he asked harshly.

"He's not your daughter's killer. He has an iron-clad alibi," Gwen said resolutely.

"But he knocked her up and fled the state. How can you think he wasn't involved?" Wright said angrily. "I want that man arrested!"

"He's already been questioned. I thought you said you didn't know any of Kathy's friends or lovers?"

"I have my resources," Wright said curtly. "I was informed about him after we spoke."

"And I heard you've been harassing him. You have no right to do that, Captain Wright."

"I have every right to speak with whomever I please! We're talking about my daughter here. How dare you talk to me like that! I will have you taken off this case immediately if—"

"Captain, we're doing everything we can to find your daughter's murderer. All I'm asking for is a little cooperation. Do you remember telling me you'd copy the files of the recent arrests for drug trafficking?"

"Yes, and here's what I have for you," he said, pulling a thin folder from his desk drawer. "I'm sure if you look up these three hoodlums, you'll have a better idea what the real world is like down there. It's vicious. It makes me sick to think my daughter was ever involved with the likes of these...this scum. I did hear that she was clean when she...when she was killed. At least that's some comfort."

"Yes, it appears she hadn't started using since she left rehab," Gwen said quietly. No thanks to you we already have that blood test result, she thought. At least Doc Maynard had drawn blood and had it shipped to the lab before the delay.

"Well, I still think that Kingley guy had something to do with it. Have your men interrogate him again."

"Like I said, we're leaving no stone unturned. By the way, do you recognize this?" Gwen asked, pulling the plastic bag with the locket out of her pocket.

"Why, yes! It's the locket I gave Kathy for her sixteenth birthday...put me back a pretty penny, but she begged me for it." His face looked gray, agonized. "Where did you find it?"

"It was taken off another murder victim. When was the last time you saw Kathy wearing it?"

"Umm…I'm not sure. Probably the last time I saw her. Maybe a week before the accident. She never took it off," he said, tearing up. "I'd like to keep it when you're through—"

"Any personal items we've found will be returned to you when we've finished our investigation," Gwen reminded him.

"It's been three days. Where the hell are you on the investigation? Are you getting close?" he nearly shouted.

"Like I said, we're examining all the evidence closely and talking with everyone who knew your daughter. We're making excellent progress," Gwen lied.

"Make sure I'm updated on that so-called progress," he said, dismissing her.

"Yes," she said on her way out.

God, that man infuriated her! He'd suffered a terrible loss, yes, but could get under her skin faster than anyone she'd ever met. She'd met many arrogant men before, but he was the king of attitude. She could feel it in the air she breathed when she was near him. It put her on the defensive, which she didn't like one bit.

As she drove back to the station, she forced the confrontation with Wright out of her mind and concentrated on meeting up with CC. It would be nice to have company working the street, and a special treat not to be teamed up with one of the guys for a change.

As she pulled into the precinct parking lot, CC was ready and waiting. She ran from the building and jumped into the passenger seat of Gwen's car.

"Perfect timing," she huffed, out of breath. "I just finished and came out for a breath of fresh air. I don't know how they can work in that stinking lab all day!"

Gwen laughed. "I suppose you get used to it when you're in it all the time."

"Not me. Like my dad, my senses are super sensitive. I can only take it so long and I need some clean air. I can smell and taste a lot of things other people can't."

"Oh? Like what?" Gwen smirked.

"Well, you know, like when chemicals have spilled or something has burned then dissipated over time. I've found that a lot of cops can't detect it after a couple days. I usually can. And when someone is cooking in my apartment building, I can usually tell you exactly what they're making, while others don't smell a thing."

"And for tastes?" Gwen asked.

"I know every spice from most countries. If I don't smell them right off, I can taste them and tell you exactly what's in the broth or gravy on your plate. If you don't believe me, you can devise a test. One of my friends poured six different sauces over pasta and I guessed the differences between every one of the dishes," CC said proudly.

"Hmm…sounds like a lot of work. I don't cook, so I'll have to take your word for it. I'm not a fussy eater and I can scarf down just about anything," Gwen teased. "But tell you what, you can combine all the best spices you can come up with and cook me dinner anytime."

"Don't think I won't do it," CC teased back, smiling.

When they parked at one of the meters on Main Street, Gwen pushed her police vehicle ID against the windshield and pulled out the file Wright had given her.

"Here's what the captain came up with for the thugs that caused trouble lately," Gwen said, opening the file for the first time.

The three men looked menacing in their mug shots. The first was a very large black man, five feet, nine inches, three hundred and fifty pounds. The second was a tall, scrawny-looking black man, six feet, two inches, and the third was a very small Mexican man, four feet, nine inches with a deep scar on his left cheek.

"That's odd," CC said, pulling a file out of her backpack. "This is the information Brad got from his contact at the North Precinct. None of those guys show up, but he's identified a gang of sixteen guys, most of which have been arrested at one time or another within the last six months. And these guys are all white," she said, handing the sheets with six mug shots each to Gwen. "Look, here's the information on all the minor drug busts during the same period. None of the names from the captain's list match."

"I'm betting that Brad's information is more accurate," Gwen remarked. "It's not unusual to find prejudice in the ranks, but Wright had to do some major digging to find these men of color. Our population is eighty-nine percent white, and since Scarletsville is so far north of any big city, the drug trade isn't as lucrative. We've attracted mostly retirees up here with ties to the old country life, so many of the kids get the heck out of here as soon as they've graduated from high school."

"That's interesting, but why would the captain try to throw us off, especially since it's his daughter and time is of the essence? And it's not like we have an army of officers to help solve this case."

"I think he's underestimated us...me anyway. I don't doubt he believes one of these men was involved in some way. I suppose he figures if I come across some big, bad boy, I'll just assume he was the perp and throw the book at him. I don't blame him for wanting to get the case closed quickly, but I'm not stopping until I find the right big, bad boy," Gwen said determinedly. "Surely he wants us to get the right guy, and maybe put some of the others in the slammer along with him."

"I'm with you. Let's go."

They talked with a couple of women standing on the corner who were trying to wave down the men from passing cars. After Gwen and CC showed their badges, the hookers clammed up and claimed to have seen nothing. They found a few other people roaming the streets, but no one who could or would offer any information. It was daylight, so the activity in the area was at a minimum. Hopefully someone from Vice could get more information during the night and early morning hours.

When they were finished circling the block and heading back to the car, they recognized a face from the mugshots they'd memorized. The heavyset black man was sitting on a porch mid-block, but stood up as they approached. He was too heavy and out of shape to try to run, and soon CC and Gwen were flanking him on either side.

"I didn't do nothing," Jaxon Thomas protested, fear evident in his expression.

"Didn't say you did," Gwen replied. "We're investigating a murder. Just wondering if you've seen anything unusual in the neighborhood."

"Nah. Same 'ol shit."

"Did you know Cyndi Jeffries?" CC asked.

"Yeah. Cyndi's one of the nice ones. God, I hope nuttin' happened to her," he said, clearly alarmed. "She lived over yonder. I paid her to babysit my kids a couple times."

Gwen told him bluntly, "She was murdered."

"Oh my God," he said, putting his large hands over his face.

Gwen gave him a few moments to compose himself and then probed, "Did you know who she hung out with?"

"She'd be pretty quiet, most the time. I never seen her with anyone, 'cept that blond woman from time to time. Come to think of it, I haven't seen her around here lately neither."

"Do you know the blond woman's name?" CC asked.

"No, just that she was pretty. Tall and kinda skinny."

"Anyone else you see with Cyndi?" Gwen asked.

"Nope. That asshole Wright tried to bust her ass a couple days ago. But Cyndi, she take no shit from nobody. I heard them arguing and he left. Didn't arrest Cyndi."

"Are you talking about Captain Wright? From the police department? You're saying he was down here?" Gwen asked incredulously.

"Yep. That's the one. He busted me a few months back. Had one of his boys take me down to the station. I was grilled for two hours, but there wasn't enough evidence I'd been selling illegal drugs. Wright told me he could make me look really bad in front of a judge, but I didn't fold and tell him what he wanted to hear like some of those other boys do. He likes to keep them on trumped-up charges to make his records look better, like they're doing their jobs real good. Hey, I'm not saying I'm any model citizen. I sold the rest of my brother's stash when I got laid off from the city. He got ten years in prison and ain't gonna be needing it no more. I gotta feed my six babies, ya know? Two damn hours of his bullshit, then Wright let me go. I jus' didn't have anything to tell him, not that I would have anyways."

"What do you do for the city?" Gwen asked.

"Dump truck driver. I move snow in winter and dirt from construction sites in summer. That son-of-a-bitch Wright would have me hauling dead bodies, if he got his way with me. No sir-eee...I didn't give him an inch. He don't like us black folk, that's for sure," Thomas said with disdain.

"You've been very helpful, Mr. Thomas. Thank you," Gwen said, handing him her card. "Please give me a call if you think of anything else."

"Yes'm."

When they reached the car, Gwen whistled softly and said, "Now isn't that interesting. So Wright's playing games to up his precinct's performance scores. I wonder what else he's been up to?"

"Yeah, that really sucks. Those poor men don't have a chance with Wright on their tails," CC commented. "What are you going to do about it?"

"For now, nothing. I can't afford to jeopardize this investigation by reporting Wright. He'll kick me off the case in a flash. But I'm sure going to record every infraction I hear about, along with all the crap he's done to screw me up, and as soon as this thing's wrapped up I'm going to the chief."

"That makes sense. He sure is making it rough on you," CC sympathized.

"Well, nothing I can do about it now. We'd better get to the precinct and see what the guys have come up with. Finding Kathy's murderer is much more important than Wright's offenses."

CHAPTER ELEVEN

Brad and Scott were waiting for them when Gwen and CC walked into the squad room. They were talking to a stranger—a tall, muscular man in his midthirties with long, straggly, light brown hair. He was wearing jeans and a baggy army jacket which was frayed at the seams.

Scott began the introductions. "Gwen and CC, this is Sergeant Tony Maglia from Vice. He's been working the downtown area longer than anyone in the department. He has several informants and knows most of the regulars in the drug trade. I think he can help us a great deal."

"Welcome." Gwen smiled, offering her hand. "We can sure use your help."

"Nice to meet you," CC chimed in.

"Hope I can get you what you need to nail the bastard responsible for your two murders," Tony offered.

"We were downtown this afternoon," Gwen said, and told them about the strange conversation they'd had with Jaxon Thomas. "Does Wright really show up in that neighborhood and harass those poor people?"

"Yep. He's been doing that for years. He thinks he's helping clean up the neighborhood, and it sure does make our precinct look good with all the arrests. But truth be known, he drives us nuts. We cringe when we see him drive up. As many arrests as he's ordered us to make, he's botched up plenty of undercover stings too. I know many of our guys have complained, but I think the brass just plays along with it now because Wright is so close to retirement," Tony informed them.

"Well, he's being a royal pain in the ass in this investigation," Scott said, outraged.

"He's not going away, so let's deal with it," Gwen proposed, surprised at the anger in Scott's voice.

"Hey, the hair found in the car is the exact match to those you found on Jeffries' body," Brad said, breaking the tension. "Now we just need a live body with the same chemistry. Sorry, no DNA, but we can prove they came from the same person. Oh, and the last person that called Kathy on her cell was the captain."

"That bastard let me think he hadn't talked to her for a week. It would make sense that Kathy had been keeping close contact with her dad, especially since she knew she needed support for her child. Keep working on the hair, Brad," Gwen ordered.

"Here's what we were able to find on the laptop," he said, handing Gwen a stack of papers approximately three inches high.

She groaned as she stuffed the papers in her briefcase. "What do you have, Scott?"

"I rechecked the car. No trailer hitch. Doesn't look like there ever was one. The bumper is smooth, no scratches. Brad had his hands full with the laptop, so I took the Holy Cross assignment. Met with a counselor by the name of..." Flipping his notebook open, Scott continued, "Marge O'Connor. She was of the opinion that Kathy was going to be successful with this intervention. It was her second time through the program, and Kathy had a positive attitude. She was doing everything she needed to do in order to stay clean. Mrs. O'Connor didn't know Kathy was dead; was really shaken up about it. Kathy told her about her pregnancy and how she really wanted to get off the drugs for good. There was no doubt in O'Connor's mind that Kathy would have been able to 'chase away her demons' this time around."

"That's so sad," CC said softly.

"Well, let's keep at it guys," Gwen said determinedly. "Good job so far, and now let's nail this monster!"

"My car's on the second-floor parking lot," CC said, walking out of the meeting with Gwen.

"I can drive you up there," Gwen offered.

"Okay. Sure."

When they got to CC's car, Gwen had an idea. She didn't want to end this day just yet.

"Hey, I've got a bottle of red wine and shrimp salad back at my place. Ah, if you're interested."

"Umm…that really sounds good. Are you sure you still want my company?"

"You bet! I can't think of anybody I'd rather be with."

***

When they got to Gwen's duplex, CC marveled to Gwen at how neat and tidy, and unusual—fascinating, was the word she used—the bungalow was. The older red brick building was divided into two large residences. Gwen's unit had two bedrooms and a spacious kitchen all in white with a sunflower border along the ceiling. There was a rustic pine built-in corner breakfast nook. Rows of copper pans and cooking utensils lined the wall above the sink. The living room was small, but comfy, with dozens of brown and beige pillows in a variety of sizes stacked in a corner and on top of the brown suede overstuffed sofa. It and a matching recliner faced a fieldstone fireplace. There were old nautical pieces everywhere; the end tables were made from brass portholes and the coffee table was a glass-covered ship's steering wheel. An antique hourglass stood on the fireplace mantel and an old propeller blade was attached to the wall above it. A floor-to-ceiling bookshelf contained a number of marine and sailing books, as well as a generous assortment of crime novels. CC was also intrigued by the numerous volumes of police, pathology and forensic science educational publications.

"This place is always quiet." Gwen spoke loudly from the kitchen. "My next-door neighbor, Pierre, is a pilot and is gone much of the time. He has a big yellow Labrador retriever, so if you see a dog, don't freak out. We put a dog door in between our two dens so Max can come and go as he pleases. He'll beg for a walk in the morning from whoever gets up first. Most of the time, Pierre pays the family down the block to feed and walk the dog when he's traveling, but we have our share of bonding time too. I always know when Pierre is gone for the night, because Max sleeps next to my bed and I nearly trip on him when I get up in the middle of the night to pee and when I get out of bed in the morning."

CC grinned. "That sounds kind of neat. It's like a community dog. It has to be the best of all worlds for him with all the 'family' members taking care of him," she commented.

"Yeah, when you meet him you'll see that he's far from neglected. He probably should lose a few pounds, but when he looks at you with those big brown eyes, you can't resist giving him a treat. He's really a gentle guy," Gwen said, bringing a tray into the living room. She had cut up cheese and sausage to put on sesame crackers, and had a bowl for each of them with romaine lettuce covered with a generous amount of shrimp and drizzled with a fragrant dressing.

"Hang on, I'll get the wine," Gwen said, hurrying back into the kitchen. She was back with a bottle of cabernet and two glasses. She lit the kindling and started a fire in the fireplace.

While they filled their plates, they started chatting about their likes and dislikes, achievements and disappointments. Gwen felt very comfortable talking with this woman, which was amazing, since she was usually very cautious when meeting someone new.

"The dressing on this salad is wonderful," CC said between bites.

Gwen looked at her and caught the deep pools of blue in her expressive eyes. "It's actually Chinese sesame oil mixed with mayonnaise. I'm glad you like it." Was it possible she was feeling the instant attraction also?

CC blushed and looked away shyly. "Everything is delicious. I hadn't realized how hungry I was," she admitted.

"I love to cook, but I'm not that good in the kitchen," Gwen said, "Besides I don't have much time for it, so I keep easy-to-prepare meals around. That way I have something decent to eat when I get home, instead of filling up with my favorite junk foods."

"Thank you," CC said when they'd finished eating. "Let me do the cleanup."

CC picked up the bowls, carefully placed them on the tray with the leftover cheese and crackers, and went into the kitchen. There were several other dishes in the sink from Gwen's preparation of the food, so she found the dish soap and filled the sink with hot water.

Gwen stood back watching, contemplating her next move. What did she have to lose, she thought. The worst that could happen would be that CC would leave and not allow Gwen to see her again outside of work. Gwen steeled herself for rejection and made up her mind to take the plunge.

As CC was still washing the dishes, Gwen came up behind her and put her arms around her. When CC turned her head, Gwen's lips met hers. She didn't resist Gwen's long, tender kiss. The electricity between them was full of passion and desire.

When they finally parted, CC said, "My God, I should wash your dishes more often!"

Gwen laughed. "Then you didn't mind?"

"Hell, no. I really like you a lot, Gwen. I wish it wasn't so late and we didn't have to be back to work so early in the morning."

"Stay for one more glass of wine. Please?" Gwen asked.

"I'd like that," CC said softly.

This time they sat on the couch holding hands and watching the burning logs die down in the fireplace. As they finished their wine, Gwen pulled CC close to her and gave her another long and passionate kiss. Her hand started stroking CC's arm, but soon found the softness of her breast. The heat of her body grew and she felt the ache and longing of her desire, yearning to take this passion to the next level.

CC pulled away slowly and said softly, "My God, Gwen. If I don't leave now, neither one of us will get a wink of sleep tonight."

"Uh-huh," Gwen said, nibbling her neck.

"Gwen…shit!"

Gwen bolted upright alarmed, and asked with concern, "I'm sorry, did I hurt you?"

"No, just the opposite. I want to take it slowly. I want it to be the right time, when we don't have to rush. I really have to go, Gwen. It's getting late. It's almost midnight. I know this is a very emotional case for you. Please, let's not rush into anything we'll be sorry for later. I enjoy working with you, and I really like you. I just—well, I wasn't prepared to get into a relationship."

"Yeah. I know. Pick you up tomorrow?"

"No, I have to go to the lab to go over more of the evidence with Charlie. I told him I'd let him know if we wanted him to run any other tests. Maybe lunch…or dinner at my place? We can talk more then."

"Both?" Gwen asked, laughing.

"Let's see how the day goes. Thanks again for the wonderful time," CC said as she rose to leave.

"Thank you," Gwen said and almost leaned over to kiss her once more after she'd helped CC into her coat and boots. She'd stopped herself just in time.

"Whew, that woman is hot!" Gwen said to herself, watching CC's car drive away.

CHAPTER TWELVE

The following day was jam-packed with following up on leads. The Chief had set up a hotline for people to call with any information regarding the two murders. They often received valuable and useful information from a hotline, but the downside was that every crackpot in the city could also call in with misleading and erroneous tips. Each bit of information had to be analyzed to make sure they weren't ignoring pertinent information.

Gwen was pleased with Chief Ziegler's decision to allow Tony Maglia to assist the task force. She also was given three more uniformed officers to follow up on the numerous calls coming in. Gwen felt they had an outstanding team with these new additions, along with Jaxon Thomas following up on anything that Vice or its informants came up with. On the downside, they were losing Jenny to one of the other teams, which was short on personnel.

Gwen picked up a stack of messages when she came into the precinct, and after making several calls, she found three that she wanted to follow up on. On her way out, she stopped at the lab and found CC deep in conversation with the chemist, Charlie Iwo, talking over something they were examining under the microscope. She pointed to her phone and CC nodded, understanding Gwen's request to call her later. They could meet up when CC was finished in the lab. Gwen waved and left the building.

Her first stop was the small pharmacy two blocks from Kathy's apartment. It appeared that Kathy had charged most of her purchases. She learned from the pharmacy records that Kathy had bought three pregnancy tests within a three-day period, about a month prior to her death. It was here also that she had filled a prescription for methadone, one of the medications prescribed for the treatment of substance abuse. This was further evidence that Kathy was taking her treatment to curb her addiction seriously. The pharmacist remembered having a lengthy conversation about the use of the drug and her pregnancy, and had advised her about other vitamins she would need to start taking regularly if she were indeed pregnant. The druggist, a robust man in his late fifties, remembered Kathy being a pleasant person, but one who seemed deeply worried about her future, especially after she had confided in him about the pregnancy.

Gwen's next stop was a good friend of Cyndi Jeffries. The woman, a tiny Asian, had a nervous habit of biting her cuticles and did so constantly as she reluctantly told Gwen that Cyndi had been happy-go-lucky until she had become friends with Kathy.

"Sure," Mindy Lei admitted, "Cyndi did hooking to earn her living, but she was generous and loving to her friends and family. She didn't take any shit from her customers, and wouldn't have anything to do with the local pimps. She was her own person. She didn't do drugs much, unless Kathy wanted to party and wanted someone to go with her to the local bars. They got free drinks and drugs from guys looking for a good time. Cyndi was quite a looker, and attracted lots of men. I went along a couple times. That Kathy was real trouble. She'd party hearty and not care who or what she did when she was high."

"Any man in particular Cyndi or Kathy spent a lot of time with?" Gwen asked.

"Lordy, yes." Mindy smiled. "Cyndi was good at what she did, and had many a repeat customer. I don't think I ever saw Kathy with the same man twice though."

"Cyndi mention anyone who got rough with her?" Gwen probed.

"Nah, she stayed away from those types. The only one I heard her complain about was that top cop man. He was related to Kathy somehow. Said he liked it rough and she'd had to put him in his place."

"Do you remember his name?" Gwen asked in surprise.

"Lady, everyone in this neighborhood knows that guy. Wright's what they call him."

Gwen grimaced, but didn't let on that she was surprised to hear the police captain was a regular customer. Gwen's blood began to simmer as she thought about how Captain Wright was taking advantage of these people for his own pleasure.

Twenty minutes later, Gwen pounded on the door in one of the tenements down the block from Cyndi's flophouse, the last place on her list. A tired-looking black man, perhaps in his eighties, shuffled to the door. Over a multicolored turtleneck sweater he was wearing a brown bathrobe cinched tightly around his waist, and worn tennis shoes without laces.

"I'm Detective Meyers, Scarletsville PD," Gwen said, showing her badge.

He slowly unclasped the safety chain and moved aside so Gwen could enter the dingy apartment.

"You called our help line indicating you might have seen something related to the murder of Cyndi Jeffries?" Gwen asked.

"Yessum," he replied.

"Can you tell me what you saw?" Gwen probed.

"Come on in and have a seat. Getcha a cup of tea."

"No thanks, uh, Mr. Davies."

"Lionel," he said, ignoring her.

He moved into the kitchen and carefully poured tea into two chipped, porcelain teacups. "Cream or sugar?"

"No, this is fine, thank you," Gwen replied, taking the seat he indicated at the rusty card table in his kitchen.

Gwen waited patiently as he poured honey into his cup, stirred, and took small sips until he was satisfied with the brew.

"What did you see that could help us?" Gwen urged.

"You know the man they call Cap'n hangs around a lot," he said slowly.

"Yes, I know," Gwen answered. "His daughter lived with Cyndi for a time."

"Always fights. Every time he come, miss. There be yelling and screaming."

"Were you in the house, or did you hear the disturbance from outside?" Gwen asked.

"I always been on the outside. I walk my dog in dis' alley behind those houses." He pointed in the direction of Cyndi's house, and then returned his attention to the living room.

Gwen noticed for the first time that a small, skinny beagle cowered under a coffee table in the next room.

"When was the last time you saw the captain at Cyndi's?"

"Day of the murder," Lionel said without hesitation.

"And did you hear them arguing that day?" Gwen probed.

"No, didn't hear nothing. Only that a car like the cap'n drives was parked in dis alley and hightailed it out fast. Next thing I know police cars everywhere."

"You're not sure it was the captain?" Gwen asked.

"No ma'am."

"Anything else?"

"You don' tell Cap'n I talk to you, hear? He make a lot of trouble for everybody. I don' need that. He destroy people, that man. He don' like you, you no find work, you no have food. They won't even serve you at grocery store."

"I promise I won't make trouble for you, Lionel. You call me if you hear anything else, okay?" she said, handing him her card.

"You nice lady. I trust. I check aroun' the neighborhood," he said slowly, looking intently at her card.

She guessed he couldn't read, but perhaps someone else would help him get in touch with her. Another glance around confirmed he didn't have a phone.

"Who called the hotline for you?" Gwen inquired.

"Hotline? What's hotline?"

"How did you get in touch with the police?"

"Oh," he said, nodding that he understood. "My son call. He big superintendent at building projects. First he don' want me involved, but I insist. He's a good boy. Has two fine sons of his own," Lionel said proudly, getting up from the table.

Lionel walked into the living room and brought back a photograph of a handsome middle-aged man, a beautiful woman with caramel colored skin, and two teenage children.

"They look like a very fine family, Mr. Davies."

"Lionel…call me Lionel. Yes, they want to do more for me, but I tell my son, you give to those children. They are our future. It's too late for me."

"Thank you for your time, Mr…uh, Lionel. I appreciate you coming forward. Please call if you have any further information," Gwen said kindly.

It was after six p.m. when Gwen arrived at the precinct, but she was the first in the squad room. She walked slowly around the room, studying the whiteboard, the timeline Brad had written up and taped to the wall, photographs of the crime scene and the mugshots of the men they'd considered suspects. The conference table was still covered with newspapers and computer printouts. Several stained Styrofoam cups had been left with portions of this morning's coffee.

CC came in a few minutes later followed by Scott, Brad and Tony.

Gwen quickly briefed them on her interviews. "It looks like Captain Wright's name comes up wherever we turn in this investigation. It appears he controls much of the action in the projects."

"Let's face it; he's a dirty cop," Scott said disgustedly. "I'd be backpedaling pretty fast by now too if I were him."

"We can't nail him for hanging around in the same neighborhood his daughter frequented," Brad offered.

"No, but we can get him for lying and impeding the investigation," CC grumbled.

"Wright hasn't done anything recently that he hasn't been doing for years," Tony chimed in. "He's always been climbing up the butts of drugs users and prostitutes. He gets his rocks off doing it, demeaning those who can't defend themselves. He backs down when anyone with muscle in the neighborhood stands up to him. The bigger the fish, the quicker Wright rabbits out of there. You should see him squirm when someone mentions the word 'lawyer.' I don't think Wright's done any harm."

"So you think it's okay for Wright to badger these poor people?" Gwen asked angrily.

"Nope. I never said it was right. It's just the way it is," Tony confessed. "You know as well as I do, Vice practically lives with these people…they dress like them, eat with them, befriend them or hate them. Easy to get hardened to that element when you live and breathe it. From what I understand, the captain grew up in Vice. He knows the neighborhood and the people… and he hates it even more knowing his daughter became a part of it."

"You're right, Tony. Thanks for reminding us what a nice guy the captain is," Gwen said sarcastically. Then she added, "Really, I appreciate your honesty and keeping things in perspective, but what the captain is doing down there gives me the creeps. I'm sorry for getting upset. I'll report what I know about the captain after we've caught our perp. I want to put him on the back burner for now and concentrate on this investigation."

"I'm with you," CC and Scott said in unison.

"Now, what else have we got?"

"I tracked Kathy's Twitter and Facebook accounts," Brad said next. "Nothing substantial, but I've been able to fill in some of the blanks as far as the 'where and who.' The tracking of Kathy's movements the past few weeks are nearly as complete as we'll be able to get them."

"I'm still pressing some of my contacts," Tony said briefly. "Nothing yet."

"I've got several leads to check up on," Scott said wearily. "The hotline's still ringing off the hook."

"Give me anything you need to follow up on," CC offered.

"So far, the cops the chief assigned have been hustling. Thanks though, I may have a few for you," he replied.

"Okay. See you all tomorrow," Gwen said, ending the meeting.

"Hey," CC said, when everyone else was gone. "I owe you dinner."

"I'd be just as happy to stop at the deli. I know you've put in a long day and I'm bushed too," Gwen said, noticing the dark smudges under CC's eyes.

"If you don't mind, I'll make it up to you another time," CC said gratefully.

"I'll take your IOU," Gwen laughed.

"Let's go to Richard's Pub. I could use a beer or two." CC smiled.

"Great!" Gwen agreed.

They had a pleasant dinner of salad, spaghetti and toasted garlic bread. They ate heartily, laughed, joked with each other. The two hours spent eating dinner and drinking two steins of beer apiece passed much too quickly. They were both exhausted when they said their goodbyes, although Gwen was still reluctant to call it a night.

Hell, Gwen thought, walking to her car, I didn't even get a kiss for dessert to end this fabulous evening!

Though she was tired to the bone, her mind was still consumed with all that was happening with the investigation. She took the copies of Kathy's e-mails that Brad had printed out to bed, and read until she felt able to sleep. But instead she recalled more of her time with Kathy. Just before Gwen had started packing up at the end of their weekend together, Kathy had urged her to stay another hour or two. Gwen still lay naked in the bed and Kathy had run out for doughnuts and coffee, so she was fully dressed. Kathy then did the most erotic striptease Gwen had ever seen. The porno flicks she'd seen didn't hold a candle to the sight of Kathy slowly gyrating in front of her and taking her clothes off slowly and sensually. It took all the willpower Gwen had to keep from leaping off the bed and tearing the rest of Kathy's clothing away from her gorgeous body. She was on fire by the time Kathy slid under the covers next to her. They'd made love passionately and furiously. Gwen's tongue had tasted every inch of Kathy's body and had brought Kathy to orgasm after violent orgasm before she was finally sated.

When her alarm awoke Gwen the following morning, the lights were still blazing and papers she had been reading were scattered, some on her bed and in a heap on the floor. She groaned, but yet was anxious to get on with her day and keep the progress moving on the investigation. Gwen felt somehow confident they would find their killer soon.

It was Friday, so maybe she could schedule their task force meeting for earlier in the day. That would give them a longer evening and maybe Gwen would finally have more time to spend with CC. They would be working this weekend, but certainly wouldn't have to get up early on Saturday morning!

CHAPTER THIRTEEN

When Gwen arrived at the precinct, she was surprised by the message that she'd been summoned to Captain Wright's office, pronto. The prior visits were her idea; she was curious to find out why he had now asked to see her.

She hurried to her car and drove across town to the North Precinct. This time, she did not have to ask for him; Captain Wright was waiting for her.

After she'd shut the door behind her, Wright tore into her. "What are you wasting your time on crap like fibers and e-mails for when we both know Jerry Kingley killed my daughter? I told you to arrest that man!"

"How do you know what we're focusing on, Captain Wright?" Gwen asked in an even tone, trying to keep her anger in check.

"I have my ways," he said haughtily.

"There's no way Jerry could have killed your daughter. He wasn't even in Wisconsin."

"You know how all those military men stick together. Do you really believe his fellow guardsmen aren't covering for him? I have information that may surprise you," Wright said smugly. He handed her three gasoline receipts.

She looked at them. They were dated the days before and after Kathy's murder.

Wright said, "You think he drove in excess of six hundred miles around the military base? He could have circled the base three hundred times in two days to put that kind of mileage on his car. Now, do you still believe Kingley was at the base while my little girl was being murdered?"

"I'll certainly look into it," Gwen said, puzzled. "Where did you get these receipts?"

"I contacted the service stations. They have the records to prove it was Jerry," Wright declared.

"I will look into this and take it into consideration," Gwen told Wright.

"Don't be pigheaded over this. I've handed you Kathy's murderer on a silver platter. Now arrest him and be done with it!"

"I'll let you know what I come up with," Gwen said, turning and walking out the door.

Snow flurries and a strong northerly wind assaulted Gwen as she left the North Precinct, but they did nothing to cool her anger. It seemed that Wright was keeping one step ahead of them in the investigation, and that meant someone on the task force was feeding him information. Could it be Brad? She hadn't known this cop for very long, but he seemed to be on the up and up. She'd worked with Scott for years, and knew he would never fold to pressure from upper echelons of the police administration. She had begun to trust CC with her deepest secrets and desires. Could CC be faking her interest in Gwen and be the mole Wright had placed on her team? They hadn't checked out Tony very well, but the chief had handpicked him for the task force. Could he be Wright's eyes and ears in the investigation? She would have to be very careful until she figured out who the guilty party was.

On the long ride back to her precinct, she decided that the fastest way to figure out who was scheming with the captain would be to confront Chief Ziegler. Maybe it was time to expose Wright and his shenanigans.

The Chief was in a meeting when she arrived at his office, but his secretary told her she could pencil Gwen in for twenty minutes at one p.m. That gave Gwen a couple hours to do a little research on the gasoline receipts Wright had given her.

Closing the door to her office, she called Jerry Kingley. He wasn't immediately available, but called back a half hour later.

"What exactly do you do for the guard?" Gwen asked.

"We're in charge of transport mostly," he told her. "We gas up and do the maintenance and repairs on the jeeps and trucks that come back to the base from the field."

"So it wouldn't be unusual for you to go through exorbitant amounts of gasoline in say, a day or two?"

"Hell, no. I've pumped two hundred or more gallons on a busy day."

"Do you fill the trucks on base?" she asked.

"Usually. But lately, with the fuel shortage, we've been using some of the local gas stations if they'll give us a discount based on volume. Depends on how full our tanks are at the time. We're instructed to keep a reserve for emergencies."

"I would think you'd keep a log as to which vehicles are serviced and how much gasoline you've put in them."

"Absolutely. We log everything we do and the gas tank readings have to balance at the end of the day with what we've disbursed. You think the government is going to believe we're not filling our own tanks at their expense? We spend more time filling out paperwork than actually doing the work that needs to be done," Jerry quipped.

"Can you fax over your records for the end of February? Say two or three weeks' worth?"

"Hey, what's this about?" Jerry asked worriedly.

"Someone came up with some gas receipts with your name on them," Gwen told him. "I just want to prove that they're related to your job. Nothing to worry about."

"Okay. Give me that number...I'll get them right over to you," Jerry said anxiously.

True to his word, Jerry's logs were on her desk within fifteen minutes. Comparing them to the three receipt copies Wright had given her, it looked as though someone had carefully forged a different license number on the copies. Jerry's receipts were not as smudged and appeared to be the original entries. Another diversion set up by Captain Wright? But why?

Gwen jotted down some notes with the facts she wanted to present to Chief Ziegler and spent the rest of the morning working through a stack of messages from the hotline. There were a lot of interesting tidbits of information floating around, but nothing significant that would require her to conduct a field audit or set up an interview.

A few minutes before one p.m., she headed to see the chief and was waiting outside his office when he arrived at twelve fifty-five. Great, an extra five minutes to bolster her case against Captain Wright.

"Good afternoon, Detective Meyers," Ziegler said, ushering her into his office. "This is a nice surprise," he said pleasantly.

Ziegler stood ramrod straight and shook her hand. He was tough with his officers, but he was fair, and probably the most honest man Gwen had ever met. He was just over six feet tall, but she'd seen him at the gym and his looks belied the strength of his body. He kept the old-fashioned brush cut from his years of military service closely trimmed, he had penetrating brown eyes, and a handlebar mustache. His deep baritone voice was perfect for the police barbershop quartet that performed at all the police family gatherings.

"I'm sorry to bother you, Chief, but I'm having a problem on the Wright/Jeffries investigation that I'd like to brief you on."

Gwen started with the newest revelation of the altered gas receipts she'd received from Wright and worked her way backward, advising him of the complaints of harassment from the downtown area. She let him know that Wright had already tried and convicted Jerry Kingley, whom she was positive was innocent.

"Every lead I get ties back to the captain in some way. I think he's trying to conduct his own investigation and trying to steer me astray so he can find the killer himself," Gwen explained. "I believe someone is feeding him information on what the task force is working on. He's always one step ahead of us and using his influence to stymie the investigation."

"This is serious, Gwen. You should have come to me sooner," Ziegler told her.

"I know and I apologize. It's just that every time I speak with Captain Wright he threatens to take me off the case. I feel I can solve these two murders given adequate time, and if we can keep Captain Wright at bay." Gwen added, "I'd have come to you sooner, but until this morning when I got the falsified receipts, I had no proof."

"Who's working on your team now?" Ziegler asked.

"There's CC, uh, Chloe Carpenter, my new partner. Sergeants Brad Wheeler and Scott Richards, and recently the man you sent from Vice, Sergeant Tony Maglia. We've got the hotline up and the uniforms you assigned—"

"Whoa. I didn't have anyone to send you from Vice yet. I was going to get Frank Matthews to you by the end of the week," Ziegler remarked. "How did this Maglia fellow get on board?"

"I don't know," Gwen said, her face reddening. "He must be our leak."

"Start meeting with the rest of your team individually or in pairs until I can get this straightened out. And, Gwen, I know I don't have to tell you not to breathe a word about this to anyone."

"Absolutely, Chief. Sorry for the mess we've got here. Now that I know who's working for Wright, I promise you nothing else will get back to him. Thank you."

"I'll be calling you in a day or two. Good work, Detective. Keep it up," Ziegler said, dismissing her.

CHAPTER FOURTEEN

When Gwen returned to her office, she canceled the task force meeting for the day and asked everyone to email their progress reports. She knew they'd grumble about the request, since that meant making a formal report on everything they'd accomplished for the day.

She spent the afternoon following up on the more promising leads from the hotline, tempted every few minutes to call CC. She so wished she could call and vent about everything that had happened, but she had promised Chief Ziegler she wouldn't tell a soul about their conversation. Besides, although it was likely that Tony Maglia was the mole Wright had planted within her task force, she didn't have any solid evidence. That meant it could still be anyone.

The afternoon flew by and at four p.m. Gwen realized she had skipped lunch. She was just grabbing her jacket when CC popped her head in the door.

"Geez, if I didn't know better, I'd think you were ignoring us." She smiled.

"Oh, hi CC. I just needed some time to clean up some loose ends. We've been flying around the city so much all week, I hadn't had time to catch up here."

"Are you on your way out?" CC asked, noticing Gwen's jacket over her arm.

"Just for a bite to eat," Gwen said, smiling.

"I know the perfect place to relax," CC said mischievously.

"Oh?" Gwen laughed.

"Follow me," CC ordered.

Twenty minutes later CC stopped her car in front of an attractive house, aluminum-sided in beige with dark brown trim. Elm and maple trees shaded half the small yard, and the bushes in front were neatly trimmed just below the front picture window.

Just inside the door they shed their coats onto an brass coat rack, and walked into a modern furnished living room decorated in bright yellows, oranges, greens and deep burgundy. To the right was a modern kitchen with a chrome and glass table in the center. The chairs were also shiny chrome, and thick hunter green and burgundy cushions were tied to the seats and backs.

"Something smells wonderful," Gwen commented.

"Have a seat and make yourself comfortable," CC told her. "I put a roast in the Crock-Pot this morning, so everything will be done in a minute."

A few minutes later they were feasting on roast beef, potatoes and carrots cooked in thick beef gravy. CC also served homemade coleslaw and rye bread. She opened a bottle of wine and filled their glasses.

"This is great! You can cook for me anytime," Gwen said, stuffing a fork full of roast beef into her mouth.

"I'm glad you like it. I like the 'quick and easy' route too."

Gwen ate until she was stuffed and pushed her plate away. "God that was good. Thank you."

"I told you I'd make you dinner. I keep my promises," she teased.

"I can't eat another bite."

"I've got dessert...homemade brownies and butter pecan ice cream. But we can wait awhile if you'd like."

"You're already spoiling me," Gwen laughed. "Let's wait."

Gwen helped CC clear the table and clean up the dishes and they retreated to the living room to finish their wine.

"Not quite the ambiance of your fireplace, but I like it here," CC said, turning on the stereo to an oldies station, which was playing soothing seventies songs.

"I like it too...and the company is fantastic," Gwen said, putting her arm around CC's shoulders. She moved slightly so their thighs touched. She knew she shouldn't be with CC, not knowing who the department leak was yet, but she couldn't help herself. This woman was intelligent, gorgeous and sexy. It had been so long since she had felt even the slightest stirring in her body for another woman.

CC turned and kissed Gwen tenderly. There was no need to hurry. Gwen returned her kiss, enjoying the feel of her soft lips and the taste of her welcoming mouth. Their passion grew and the sensual melding of their bodies turned more desperate. CC finally pulled away and stood, grasping Gwen's hand and leading her into the bedroom.

Gwen followed CC's leisurely pace as they undressed each other. God, she's beautiful, Gwen thought when they were finally standing at the end of the bed naked. CC took Gwen's hand again and led her to the side of the bed. She pulled down the covers and slid between the silky sheets. Gwen followed and snuggled closely to CC, wanting to feel every inch of the body next to hers and take in the scent of her perfume and the musky odor of her desire.

Gwen slowly and tenderly caressed CC's breasts until her nipples were rigid under her fingertips. They kissed until passion led to urgent desire. She carefully traced her fingers down her firm belly, gradually and deliberately drawing small, titillating circles with her touch, and then finally lowered her hand between CC's thighs. She massaged the tiny hardness between her legs, feeling the moistness of her desire. When she could wait no longer, Gwen plunged her fingers into CC until she arched and screamed with orgasm.

Massaging CC's inner thigh, she was planning on pleasuring her again. CC pushed her hand away.

CC scooted her body down and buried her head between Gwen's legs. Lightly and sensually, she sucked on her clit until Gwen was close to orgasm. Just as Gwen thought she was going to explode, CC thrust her fingers into Gwen's welcoming body and Gwen experienced the most gigantic, powerful orgasm she'd ever experienced. "Oh my God," Gwen cried.

They rested in each other's arms until they were again full of raw desire, and then began their sensual dance all over again; tasting, exploring, and finding each other's most sensitive spots. Gwen thought she'd never get enough, so infatuated she was with CC's body and the thrill of her seductive touch. Their bodies felt perfectly matched as they intertwined their bodies together.

Exhausted from their lovemaking, CC laid her head on Gwen's shoulder. Gwen gently ran her fingers along CC's arm, back and forth rhythmically until they fell asleep, still entwined together.

CHAPTER FIFTEEN

Gwen awoke to the sound of her cell phone. Disoriented, it took her several moments to remember where she was. Lying next to her was CC, rubbing her eyes and trying to figure out where the strange sound was coming from.

Gwen jumped out of bed, found her jeans, and flipped her phone open.

"Geez, Gwen. It's nine thirty a.m. I've called your house a dozen times looking for you," Scott said, irritation evident in his voice.

"Last I remember, it's Saturday. I sleep in on Saturdays, Scott," she said with a hint of anger in her own voice.

"Yeah, okay. Sorry, but Jerry's back in town. He arrived last night to start packing up his shit before he moves to Illinois. Wright is still harassing him, and I thought you might want to talk to him."

"Sure. I would like to chat with him before he moves out of town. How long will he be around?"

"He said he'd be out of here as soon as he's packed. Sometime this afternoon, I guess," Scott informed her.

After writing down the address, Gwen said, "Thanks, Scott. I appreciate your letting me know."

"Sure, boss," he said lightheartedly and disconnected.

"What was that all about?" CC said sleepily.

"I'm going to have to meet with Jerry Kingley in a while," Gwen said conspiratorially, "but not before I finish what I started last night."

She jumped on the bed and started tickling CC until they were both laughing and wrestling under the covers. Their horseplay soon turned serious and they made love again.

"That's one hell of a way to wake up in the morning," CC said hoarsely.

"Umm…that's the way I like to wake up too, and if I didn't have to work, we'd still be in bed at dinnertime."

"I'd like to go with you to speak with Jerry," CC said.

"I'd appreciate your input. Besides, I like your company and you are my partner," Gwen said, leaning over and giving CC another passionate kiss.

"You're right. We'd better get up now or we never will get out of bed today." She kissed Gwen again quickly, jumped out of bed, and ran to the bathroom.

They made a quick stop for coffee and breakfast sandwiches before hopping on the freeway and were on their way by eleven a.m. Gwen estimated it was about an hour's drive to the resort area where Jerry lived.

Most of the snow had melted and the fields along the highway were starting to show their deep green growth. Magnolia trees were starting to bloom with tiny white and pink flowers. The air smelled fresh and clean in the crisp country air, and they were able to crack the car windows open for the first time since winter had begun.

The two women chatted about family and friends, and Gwen's hand rested on CC's thigh as she drove. They learned more about each other's likes and dislikes in food, music and movies. Gwen was almost sorry to arrive at their destination; they'd had so much fun talking and laughing with each other.

As they pulled onto the long country road spotted with tiny cottages and campsites, they recognized a Scarletsville unmarked police car about two houses down from Jerry's address. Just as they parked, Gwen's cell phone rang.

"Gwen, I'm on my way," Scott told her, "but I've been having trouble with my phone reception along these old country roads. I'm about two miles away. Jerry just called saying that Wright was trying to break into his cabin."

"We just pulled up," Gwen told him. "We're going in now."

"Be careful," Scott warned.

"We will. Hurry and call for more backup," she said before signing off.

"You take the rear," Gwen told CC, removing her revolver from her shoulder holster. "And be extremely careful."

When CC was out of sight around the side of the building, Gwen crept slowly and stealthily up the porch steps. The screen door was half off its hinges and the inner door was wide open. As she brushed past the entranceway, the screen door let loose, breaking the last hinge and falling to the ground with a resounding crash.

Just inside the door Gwen stopped, her weapon held steady. She saw Wright leaning over Jerry's prone body. Wright had his service revolver in one hand and a butcher knife in the other, poised to stab Jerry in the jugular. Blood was pouring from Jerry's right kneecap. Wright had apparently shot him to keep him from getting away. He had two stab wounds; one approximately two inches below his right shoulder blade and the other to the right of his ribcage. Wright's hand with the knife stopped midair.

"What the hell are you doing here?" Wright barked. "Drop your gun or I'll shoot," he said. She heard a click as he cocked the gun, forcing a round of ammunition into the chamber.

Gwen dropped her gun. "You'll never get away with this, Captain."

"Hell I won't," he replied.

"Why?" she asked softly. The question was encompassing.

"I didn't mean to kill Kathy," he gasped. "I wanted her to clean up her act. I begged her to move back home. I grabbed her by the shoulders to shake some sense into her and she spit in my face. She'd lost all respect. I was her father!"

Gwen could tell he was no longer talking to her, but reliving the scene of his daughter's death. Tears were streaming down his face.

"I didn't mean to kill her, but she spit in my face, I lost it. I put my hands around her neck, but I never meant to kill her. I cleaned her up after...after the argument. I didn't know what to do until the snow started falling and I staged the accident. What else could I do? I was sure no one would question her losing control of her car around that curve in the icy weather..." Then his face turned red with rage, and he seemed to return to reality. "Until you started nosing around! You couldn't leave well enough alone, could you!" he screamed.

"And Cyndi?" Gwen asked.

"She knew too much. She was there when I dragged Kathy out of that...that pigsty and took her home. Jerry," he continued, glancing down at the man at his feet, "I hate him for what he did to my little girl. He's scum just like the rest of them. He doesn't deserve to live, and neither do you!"

Wright aimed his gun at Gwen's head. She froze in terror.

A gunshot sounded and Gwen dropped to her knees but it was Wright who crumpled to the floor. He hadn't gotten his shot off. CC rushed from behind him and quickly cuffed his hands behind his back while he was still stunned. Blood spurted from his right shoulder.

"You won't get away with this," Wright screamed. "They'll never believe you!"

"Oh yeah?" Gwen pulled her keychain out of her pocket and clicked the rewind button on the tiny tape recorder. Seconds later Wright's voice filled the room, "I didn't mean to kill her..."

Wright's face turned white and he winced in pain, pulling hard against his handcuffs.

Gwen scrambled to Jerry. He was still breathing. She pulled out her phone to call for backup just as Scott ran through the door with a half dozen uniformed officers.

CHAPTER SIXTEEN

"Excellent work, Sergeant," Chief Ziegler congratulated her. "I know you've already taken the exams for lieutenant. Having this case in your record will do nothing but help you."

"Thank you, Chief. I appreciate it," Gwen replied.

"It took a lot of guts to do what you did. I'm the first to admit, not all of us wearing the uniform are cut out to be cops. Along the line I've seen men and women succumb to temptation, start out bending the rules a little bit, take a couple bribes, get greedy. That's why, when I see someone with the stamina and dedication you and your team exhibited, you deserve promotion."

"Just doing my job," Gwen said modestly.

"Well, we've got a ways to go, but I just wanted to let you know how much I appreciate the work you've done. Stanley Wright is still in the hospital with the shoulder wound and isn't talking, except to his lawyer. CC's clear, her discharge of her weapon has already been judged as tactical, a good shooting. You'll be testifying at the trial and it's bound to be a three-ring circus, knowing Stanley as I do. Tony Maglia is suing for wrongful termination, even though we have plenty of infractions in his file. Seems he's prone to taking bribes from both the supposedly 'good guys' and the bad ones. We raided a storage locker rented in the name of one of his aliases, and found just about everything we were missing from the evidence room," Ziegler said, shaking his head in disgust. "We even have surveillance footage of him coming out of the unit. Still he thinks he can sue, the greedy bastard! No matter how long I'm on the job, I never cease to be amazed."

"That's what keeps us going, Chief," Gwen laughed. "Keeps us young, eh?"

"You maybe," he laughed with her. "Me, I just lose another patch of hair on the top of my head. Too late for gray hairs. I've barely got any left to comb now."

When Gwen left Chief Ziegler's office, she was exuberant, and couldn't wait to tell CC the good news. Gwen checked the lab first. Finally, after taking the stairs down to the ground floor, she saw CC coming into the revolving doors.

"Hey!" Gwen called.

"Hey yourself! What are you beaming about?" CC asked.

"Ziegler's recommending me for lieutenant. I want to celebrate!"

"Congratulations! That's great! And you deserve it with as hard as you work. Where do you want to go?"

"I know a nice, cozy restaurant where we can ravish a huge porterhouse steak and the best baked potatoes in town. They've got a superb salad bar too," Gwen beamed. "And afterward…"

"I can ravish you," CC finished her sentence.

"That's exactly what I had in mind!"

"I have to take these samples up to the lab and I'll be ready to go," CC said, hurrying off.

An hour later they were sitting at a back table in Seventh Heaven Restaurant, watching the sun set on Lake Walleye.

"This is a nice place," CC said, looking around at the rustic atmosphere. There was a mounted moose head over the main entryway, a bear bust over the restrooms, and numerous stuffed fish decorating the walls.

"This is my favorite place. I like my meat and potatoes, and they serve the best steaks in town," Gwen replied.

They both ordered the porterhouse steaks with baked potatoes and helped themselves to the salad bar. While they were eating, CC asked softly, "Have you ever been in love?"

"Yeah," Gwen admitted thoughtfully. "I'd always admired Kathy from afar…almost envied her for her wild ways and hearty spirit. Then we had that wonderful weekend, and I thought, this is it. I fell hard and way too quickly. When I returned home Kathy avoided me for a few days, then returned one of my many messages and said she was engaged to one of the jocks from school. Of course, I was crushed. I don't think I ever did stop loving her. I had a hard time resolving why we couldn't stay together, and I couldn't put the hurt behind me for a long time afterward. I finally realized Kathy was all about appearances. I mistook our lovemaking for her caring about me, when all it came down to was another 'adventure' Kathy could chalk up to her 'experiences.'"

They ate in silence for a few minutes before Gwen continued, "Then I started dating someone on the force. She was just a year behind me in the academy. We were hot and heavy for seven or eight months. We'd just started planning a future when a drunk driver hit her. A guy pulled out in front of her, plowing through a stop sign despite the flashing lights on her squad. The accident killed both of them instantly."

"I'm so sorry, Gwen. That must have been hard."

"Yeah, I was messed up over it for a while. What about you? Tell me about your loves."

"I lived with a woman for two years. We had what I thought was a beautiful relationship, liked to do the same things and spent every moment we could together. That is, when her work didn't interfere. She was a schoolteacher. She taught second graders.

She could have been fired if the school officials found out she was gay, and heaven knows what would have happened if some of her students went to their parents with that information. I finally got sick of sitting home alone when she went to the school functions …picnics, day trips and overnighters, awards ceremonies…there was always something she was running off to. Hell, she wouldn't even go to a movie theatre with me for fear of being recognized, but she had a heavy social calendar when it came to her school buddies.

"I remember one time when I took her grocery shopping. The cart was piled full and it was her turn to buy. She saw one of her kids with his mother coming up to the checkout line where we stood, and she just bolted…walked away and out the door. I was panicked since I didn't have my wallet with me, but as they came up, I offered them a place in line ahead of me. They were only carrying a few items and I figured it would give me time to figure out what I was going to do. By the time my load was rung up and bagged, Judy was back. But I never totally forgave her. She was so damn paranoid and could never admit who she really was. She was too scared to come out in the open and I couldn't continue to live like that."

"We've both had some healing to do," Gwen said softly.

They walked slowly back to Gwen's car. It was now completely dark and the parking area had emptied except for a few cars along the opposite side of the lot. Gwen leaned over and kissed CC tenderly. CC returned the kiss and slid closer. Gwen slid her hand into CC's jacket and massaged her firm breasts, then moved her hand lower and unzipped her jeans. She slipped her hand down until she could massage the moist mound between her thighs. CC cried out almost immediately, grinding her torso against Gwen's hand.

When they parted, Gwen laughed and said, "I'll never be able to drive home unless we clean off these steamed up windows."

"You wouldn't be blaming me for that, would you?" CC giggled.

"Hmm…is this one of those 'damned if you do, and damned if you don't' questions?" she asked, turning on the ignition and switching the defrosters on full blast.

They held hands and talked while they waited for the windows to clear.

"Are you afraid of facing Wright in court?" CC asked.

"Hell, no. We've got enough evidence to nail his ass good, even without the confession I taped. Brad got a sample of his hair when he was booked, and is sure he can match it to the samples we collected. The rest of the fibers I'm sure can be matched when they finish examining Wright's house and car."

"I've never been comfortable in court, facing the accused with a jury," CC confessed. "I envy you being so comfortable with it."

"You'll get used to it. The first few times were scary, I'll admit. But I don't get rattled easily anymore. Besides, I think we have a super good team now. If there's any evidence to be found, we'll have it to bolster our case. I think it's only when you get sloppy and don't have all your ducks in order that you get in trouble…and when you allow the opposing attorney to badger you without throwing his bullshit right back at him."

"I suppose you're right. I've had to testify only three times, and each time after a sleepless night. I'd practically forgotten my own name by the time I was called to the stand." CC laughed.

"I'm sure you do just fine," Gwen said, putting the car in gear and driving out of the parking lot. "By the way, we should have all the loose ends tied up in a couple days. What do you think about going to the Wisconsin Dells for an overnighter? We could rent a cabin and take in all the sights. It should be beautiful this time of year, and we certainly could use a couple days of vacation."

"I'd like that. It would be great to get out of town for a while."

"I'll check with Brad and Scott tomorrow to make sure the schedule is clear, and then I'll make our reservations," Gwen said happily.

CHAPTER SEVENTEEN

The next day in the squad room Gwen barely had a chance to take off her coat and pour a cup of coffee before Chief Ziegler's secretary called and asked if she could come right up to his office.

When she arrived, he was waiting for her. "Good morning, Chief," she said cheerfully.

"Good morning, Lieutenant. Good to see you again," he said. Gwen could tell he was troubled. "I know you still have to wrap up your last case and have a trial to prepare for, but I need you and your team to jump in on this investigation as soon as you can...meaning yesterday." He handed her a thick folder labeled The Dive.

Ziegler continued, "Three of their regular patrons, women, have disappeared within the past week. I thought you and Detective Carpenter would be able to infiltrate the scene easier than anyone else. It's a rough crowd though, so you'll have to be cautious. The name Dive describes it accurately, from what I hear. It's a local beer joint catering to a biker crowd. They sponsor dart and pool leagues, and we've had several incidents of roughhousing in the past, but nothing like this. These three women just vanished. No one has seen or heard from them since they left the premises."

"I'll get right on it, Chief," Gwen said, wondering whether the women were lesbians.

Walking out she thought about the plans she and CC had been making to get out of town. Their mini-vacation would have to wait. She was sorry to have to disappoint CC, but she would make it up to her another time.

When she returned to her office she called her team together to work out a game plan.

"Time to get out your leathers," Gwen joked.

It was decided that Gwen would go into The Dive first and CC would enter a half hour later. They would pretend not to know each other and see who in the crowd was talkative. They needed to determine if anyone could relay any information about the disappearances, the missing women themselves, or any other relevant facts. Scott would keep surveillance on the outside of the bar with a team of two other plainclothes men the chief had authorized. Brad would be available to tail anyone of interest. Their schedules would change from days to the night shift, so Gwen dismissed everyone to catch some shuteye before taking their positions at eight p.m.

When only CC was left in her office, Gwen apologized for the change in plans.

"Things happen. Don't worry about it. It did seem too good to be true, didn't it?" CC smiled.

"We will go another time. I promise," Gwen said, relieved CC was taking the news so well.

"I'll hold you to that," she laughed, saluting Gwen.

"Better get some rest. I'll see you at around eight thirty. Be careful," Gwen cautioned. "I'd love to be at your side, but I'm afraid we wouldn't get as much done. If you need to contact me, text me from the ladies' room or from your car. Scott will be waiting in the parking lot if we need backup. Don't take any unnecessary chances."

"You be careful too," CC said and kissed Gwen quickly on the lips. "See you tonight!"

Gwen left the office about ten a.m. and headed home. She took the thick file Ziegler had given her to read. The three missing women were Meg Daniels, twenty-three years old, black, four foot eleven inches, ninety-five pounds, described as very sociable, last seen leaving The Dive; Carole Planton, thirty-eight years old, white, five foot five inches, one hundred thirty pounds, quiet, weight lifter and motorcycle enthusiast, last seen leaving The Dive; and Amy Farley, twenty-seven years old, white, five foot ten inches, one hundred ninety pounds, very outspoken, last seen leaving The Dive.

It was noon before she set her alarm for six p.m. and lay down for a nap. Cuddled up with her pillow, she dreamed about the lost weekend she had planned with CC.

When the alarm went off, Gwen woke up with a smile on her face. She showered quickly and dressed in black jeans, black leather boots, a beige turtleneck sweater and threw her brown leather jacket onto the chair next to the door. Inspecting herself in the mirror, she nodded. She would fit right in. She wasn't very hungry, but she forced herself to eat a can of chicken noodle soup with some saltine crackers.

At seven thirty she was ready to go. She'd be a little early, but she was antsy to get this investigation under way.

CHAPTER EIGHTEEN

Gwen made it to The Dive by seven fifty. Scott was already in the parking lot. She pretended not to notice him, but from the corner of her eye she caught him winking at her as he continued drinking from a large Styrofoam cup.

Inside, The Dive was dark. She stood in the doorway for a few moments, blinking until her eyes adjusted to the dingy atmosphere. It stank of stale cigarette smoke and beer, and her eyes stung as she moved to the bar and sat on one of the chrome and red plastic barstools. The bartender had his back to her. He was tall and skinny, had a shaved head, and when he turned around she saw dark stubble covering his face. His T-shirt was red with a bull's-eye under the words The Dive. There were only two other men at the bar, and they were in deep conversation with the bartender.

The surface of the countertop had once been white with gold specks, but was now deeply gouged and stained. Above the shelves of bottles of booze on the far wall was a large Miller Brewing mirror. Catching Gwen's eyes in the mirror alerted the bartender he had another customer.

"Help you?" he said, eyeing her up and down, scrutinizing her too closely and giving her a creepy feeling.

"What do you have on tap?" she asked.

"Miller. Just about anything in bottles."

"I'll take a tap Miller Light."

"Just Miller."

"Huh?" she asked.

"The spigot for the Light ain't working. I can give you a bottle."

"That'll work." She tried to squelch her exasperation.

"Be a buck fifty," he said, opening the bottle and plopping it down in front of her with a dirty cardboard coaster and water-stained glass.

Gwen threw a five-dollar bill on the bar.

"Ain't safe, you being all alone and all. Had a bit of trouble here of late."

"Oh?" Gwen asked.

"Three women disappeared in the past week. Not a trace since they left here."

"Do I look like I can't take care of myself?" she said, showing some bravado.

"Not the point. One of them that's missing was a big girl. Looked like she could handle herself too."

"And the other two?" she egged him on.

"Meg was tiny. But she was a black spitfire when you got her going." He laughed at his memory of her. "Carole was medium. About your size, but she could hold her own too. Had a big Harley some of the guys couldn't even handle. We put it up in the shed when she disappeared, so's no one would swipe it."

One of the men at the end of the bar joined in. "Carole lifted weights. Used to arm wrestle for her drinks and just about always won." He was a burly fellow with short gray hair and tattoos covering his arms.

"Amy was an Amazon," the other man offered. He had a deep, gravelly voice and a bad smoker's cough, and was not quite as big as his partner. "She was big-boned, about six feet. Man, how'd someone grab her off the street without her raising holy hell and waking up the neighborhood, I'll never figure out."

"Dunno," the partner replied, shaking his head.

"I'll be careful," Gwen said, taking a sip of her beer. Their descriptions matched the profiles she'd read, so she knew the men were being on the up and up with her.

"Yeah, well you just make sure you have one of the guys walk you to your car when you leave," the bartender said gruffly.

"My name's Gwen," she said, extending her hand.

"Whatcha doing in a place like this anyway," he answered, taking her hand. "I'm Ben, and those two roughnecks over there are Jimmy and TJ."

"Uh, I just moved into the neighborhood. Heard I could find some competition for a mean game of darts," she said, pulling the leather case out of her pocket with her tungsten diamond cut darts and slapping them onto the bar.

Jimmy let out a nasally snort. "You looking for a game, you'll have all the challengers you'd want around nine."

"We got some real championship players," TJ piped up proudly. "Made the all-state tournament in 2009. Came in second, but that's just 'cause them judges were prejudiced."

"Then I guess I'm in the right place," Gwen said smugly just as the door opened and CC walked into the bar.

"Man-o-man," Ben groaned. "We're gonna have our hands full tonight, fellas."

"Excuse me?" CC asked quizzically, choosing a stool in the middle of the bar, well away from any other patrons. Gwen couldn't help staring at the change in her appearance. She had her long blond hair tied back in a ponytail and was wearing a black silk blouse, black jeans and black blazer. Her boots had two-inch heels making her look much taller than her five-foot height.

"I was just explaining to this other gal how we've had some crime around here," Ben explained.

"Okay," CC said, unconcerned.

"Well, it's just that we don't know if it's safe for a single woman like yourself to be hanging here right now," Ben tried to explain diplomatically.

"Guess I'll be the judge of that. You got Tanqueray back there?" she demanded. "I'll have a gin and tonic."

Jimmy and TJ started laughing. "She's a tiger, Ben. You'd better be careful," they joked.

"Here you go." A red-faced Ben put her drink in front of her. "I'm gonna call you Scorpion."

"Call me anything but darlin' and we'll get along just fine," CC replied, drawing laughter from the rest of the group.

"So what brings you in here?" Ben demanded.

"Pool, darts and some good company, if it's any of your business," she replied saucily.

Ben didn't have time to reply, as just then a group of eight men and women shuffled in and he busied himself filling their drink orders. Others began sauntering in the door in groups of two and three, and by nine p.m. the bar was packed.

Gwen joined a group gathering for a game of darts, while CC moved toward the pool tables in the back of the room.

Gwen played three games of darts with a dozen other people and won two out of the three. The conversation revolved around the disappearances of the three women; everyone was generally still reeling from the shock of learning their friends had vanished, and were open about sharing their impressions of them. Amy was the least liked of the three. She was depicted as outspoken and opinionated, and her large stature reinforced her "take no prisoners" approach to life. The petite Meg was clearly everyone's favorite. The small black woman had been friendly and sympathetic to all, and was someone everyone went to when they needed a shoulder to cry on. The group didn't know much about the quiet Carole, other than her passion for weight lifting and Harley motorcycles. She had most often kept to herself and played a little pool, but never darts.

CC had put four quarters on the rim of the pool table, waiting for her turn to challenge the winner, but passed on her turn when she got involved in a deep discussion with a grossly obese black woman named Reyna. Reyna didn't join in the billiard games, but clearly was the busybody of the joint. Everyone greeted her warmly as they came to the tables, and she had personal comments for each of them to elicit the latest on their love lives, or any other significant challenges they'd been confronted with since she last saw them. She sat in a battery-powered scooter parked close to one of the small tables nearest the pool tables.

"What makes no sense," Reyna whispered in a thick, Louisiana drawl, "is that none of these gals was in the profession, you know? I could see if they was hookers or druggies, but we don't cater to them types in here. Jus' about all of the folk that hangs here got jobs and families."

"How well did you know these women?" CC asked.

"'Bout as well as anybody else here, I'd guess. Carole didn't talk to a lot of people, but she joined in back here on occasion. She worked two jobs, so was usually half dead when she came in…oops, didn't mean to say it like that. She put all her money into that hog she rode, and I think she was in over her head. Everyone was friends with Meg. You know the type. Has that personality that everyone loves and tiny figure that makes you want to hug her to death. Shit, didn't mean to say that neither!

"Amy was, well, just Amy. She had the habit of sticking her foot in her mouth and getting folk pissed off at her. Don't think she meant to be so mean, but people—the men mostly—took it wrong. Wasn't nobody going to change her mind when it was made up, Lordy no! Guess what they'd get riled up about mostly was Amy sticking her nose into everyone's beeswax and thinking she knew better than they did."

"What do you think happened to them?" CC asked.

"I was thinkin' they all got killed somehows, but don't tell anyone I said that. Most the guys are feeling real bad they didn't protect the womenfolk here better. I jus' don' see that all three of them would quit coming around just that quick. Don' make no sense to me…none at all."

"Well, I didn't know any of them, but I'm hoping for the best. Maybe all three decided to take a couple weeks off…just get away from everything for a while," CC suggested.

"I hope you're right. Now what's your story, young lady?"

"Huh…uh, me?" CC said, deep in thought about the missing women.

Reyna looked around them, and then laughed, "Duh. Who'm I talking to?"

"Uh, I'm a customer service rep for Wisconsin Mutual Funds. I do mostly telephone sales from home. It's pretty boring, so I decided I needed to get out more. A person gets stir-crazy after doing that ten hours a day, every day," CC improvised.

"Don' I know that! Lordy! 'For I got this motorized cart, I'd sit home alone for hours watching the TV. Used to be able to tell you who was doing what with who on all the soaps. I got a couple grown boys, but they keep busy with their own families…don' want to be bothered with their ol' mama."

They chatted for a while longer and Reyna filled CC in on some of the other patrons as they watched them play pool. Just after midnight, CC started yawning and excused herself, promising to come back for a visit the following evening.

Walking from the table, she glanced over and noticed that Gwen was still sitting at the bar. Before she was able to walk out the door, Ben noticed her and yelled to TJ to walk CC out to her car. CC saw Gwen from the corner of her eye, and was sure she detected a wink and slight smile as she left with TJ at her heels.

By one a.m. The Dive was practically deserted, with only a few stragglers left at the bar. Gwen had drunk only three beers in the five hours she'd been at the bar, and was still running on nervous energy and adrenaline from the intense dart matches she'd joined. It was obvious she had already talked to everybody she would be able to pump for information tonight. Besides, her thoughts kept drifting back to CC wearing that sexy black blouse under the blazer. Gwen wondered if she was still awake.

Gwen said her goodbyes and Ben stopped his cleanup and walked her out, leaving the other patrons on their own until Gwen had locked her car doors and started her engine.

She rolled down her window. "Thanks, Ben. I had a great time tonight."

"Good. You'll be back then. Can always use the business."

Gwen dialed CC's number as soon as she had driven out of the parking lot.

"Hello there!" CC answered cheerfully.

Gwen laughed. "You must have enjoyed a nice nap earlier to be this chipper in the wee hours of the morning."

"Yeah, I slept pretty well after leaving the office this morning. Guess I need it, but now I'm wide awake. I'm still trying to write my report regarding the information I got at The Dive. I don't want to forget anything and I was lucky enough to hear most of the bar's gossip. Reyna knew everybody and everything they were up to," CC said, exasperated. "I feel like I've been frequenting there for years, and I just don't know how much of it is relevant to our case."

"Want some help?" Gwen asked hopefully.

"If you don't mind, I'd love it. I can put on a pot of coffee if you'd like. This may take awhile," CC said.

"I sure hope so," Gwen said to herself, then to CC, "Be there in about twenty minutes. Yeah, coffee sounds great."

Gwen turned up the volume of her car stereo and started singing along to the oldie "Do You Believe in Magic" by the Lovin' Spoonful.

CC was pacing anxiously at the door when Gwen arrived. "I just don't know how to write this report," she whined.

"Let's take a look," Gwen offered. CC poured her a cup of coffee and the two shared the information they'd been able to obtain at The Dive.

Their stories meshed fairly well, and Gwen started typing in the missing pieces from her recollection. It didn't take her long to fill in the remaining information and complete CC's report. It was just past three a.m. when she finished, and turned to find CC sound asleep on her sofa, snoring softly. She got up and covered her with an afghan, rinsed her coffee cup and turned off the pot, and quietly left, locking the door behind her.

Gwen jumped in the shower soon after arriving home, trying to wash the smell of The Dive out of her hair and off her body.

Then she put on her flannel pajamas, made some strong herbal tea and went to bed. She made several notes to include in her own report, and finally turned the light out at nearly five a.m.

It had been a long, tiring day, but she lay awake for a long time thinking about CC. In hindsight, she wished she had cuddled up next to CC on the couch and had not left. She already missed her, and her emotions were taking over way too quickly. Maybe this is the one, she thought as she finally drifted off into a restless sleep.

CHAPTER NINETEEN

Gwen got out of bed at eleven a.m. There was a task force meeting at noon, and she had to hurry. She hadn't set the alarm, thinking she would sleep only a couple of hours.

With no time to make coffee, she grabbed a bagel from the refrigerator to eat on the way. God, she hated to rush. She hoped the day improved as it progressed.

Gwen made it to her office at exactly 12:07 p.m. Everyone else had already arrived and was sitting around chatting amicably. "Sorry I'm late," she gasped, still out of breath. "What do we have so far?"

CC, who looked refreshed and alert, told them all that she had learned from Reyna the previous night. Then Gwen read the additional notes she'd jotted down, filling them in on the details The Dive's patrons had recalled about the women, including their theories about what could have happened to them.

"No one thinks they took off on their own accord," CC added. "I get the impression they don't expect to see these women alive again."

"Exactly the impression I got," Gwen agreed.

"There was no one hanging around outside last night," Scott told them. "Everyone who drove into the lot went right into the bar, and drove away when they left. I spent a few minutes checking the back lot and bushes, but didn't see any evidence of someone lurking around or having set up a vantage point to watch the comings and goings of those going into the bar; no footprints or scuffle marks anywhere close to the parking lot. I even checked to see if someone had climbed a tree, but those are old pines in the back, and they'd have needed a ladder to get up into them."

"I was circling the neighborhood," Brad informed them. "It was a quiet night. Didn't appear anyone was out that didn't have business being there."

"Did you get the warrants to search the missing women's apartments?" Gwen asked.

"Yep. Got them right here," Brad said, holding up a manila envelope.

"Okay, we'll split up in groups. CC, you go with Brad to Meg's place. Scott, you're with me at Amy's, and we'll all meet at Carole's to compare notes. First team that gets there can start the search."

Nods all around confirmed everyone was comfortable with the arrangement, and they filed out to begin their assignments.

CC caught up to Gwen before they reached the elevators and whispered, "I'm sorry I fell asleep on you last night."

"Don't worry about it. Anything as wonderful as being with you is worth waiting for," Gwen whispered back.

"Catch you later then, and thanks for finishing my report!"

When Gwen and Scott got to Amy's apartment, the place was nearly empty and looked as though a transient had made her home in the place. They found a single mattress on the bedroom floor and a couple of overturned boxes that were being used for tables. Clearly, Amy's apartment was her last priority and lowest on her list of expenditures. There was no phone or computer, and only a few clothes in the closet that were large women's sizes. There was very little food in the tiny kitchen.

"Looks like we're spinning our wheels here," Gwen said. "Let's give it to the crime scene techs to check for blood and head over to Carole's."

"I'm with you on that," Scott said. "That's the worst, or I should say least, lived-in apartment I've seen. Did she just move in?"

"Lease says she moved in six months ago. She obviously only cared about somewhere to sleep and didn't bother decorating," Gwen replied, firing up her car.

Carole's place was only ten blocks away, so they were there in less than five minutes.

They walked up two steps to the porch of an old but well-kept little house. It was painted a garish yellow, but the bushes were trimmed and the yard looked well kept. At the door, Gwen turned around and signaled Scott to keep quiet. The screen door was ajar and the inside door was wide open. Drawing her weapon and moving slowly and quietly, she inched into the house. There was a teenager in baggy clothes with his back to her leaning over a drawer of some kind.

"Police. Stop and put your hands over your head," Gwen ordered.

The boy jumped and cried out, throwing his hands up over his head, "I'm her brother for God's sake! Don't shoot!"

"Take your wallet out of your pocket with two fingers of your left hand and kick it over to me," Gwen told him.

He carefully complied, pulling out a black wallet with his thumb and index finger, dropping it on the floor and giving it a hearty kick in her direction. The wallet skidded on the threadbare carpeting and Gwen stuck out her shoe to stop it. She opened it and looked at the picture ID. It read, Thomas J. Planton. The same last name as Carole's.

"What the hell are you doing here?" Gwen demanded.

"She's got thousands of dollars in tools here. I wanted to make sure no one stole them," he said weakly.

Gwen scowled. "More like you wanted to steal them before someone else did."

When he moved slightly to the left, she noticed he'd been riffling through a Craftsman 8-drawer tool chest on wheels. It was similar to the one she had in her own garage, so she knew it was worth plenty.

"I've got two other brothers. Just wanted my share. Trying to avoid the family fight, you know?"

"Empty your pockets on the floor, and do it now," she ordered. "You're going to have to wait until this stuff has been examined by the crime unit and released to the—" she emphasized the word—"family."

"Aw, shit!" he muttered, emptying his pockets and laying screwdrivers, clamps and wrenches on the floor in front of him.

The boy couldn't have been eighteen, and was wearing a gray flannel shirt and baggy bib overalls with deep pockets, giving him plenty of room to hide his stolen tools.

"See, you've already destroyed evidence by putting your fingerprints on those," she barked.

"I did?" Thomas looked shocked and turned beet red. "Uh, I'm sorry. I didn't think…"

"No, you didn't think. Now get the hell out of here and don't come back until we're finished."

"Yes, ma'am," he blurted, and bolted out the door.

When he was gone, Gwen and Scott burst out laughing.

"You nearly had that kid peeing in his pants," Scott said.

"Yeah, did you see him start shaking when I told him he got his fingerprints on those tools?" Gwen chuckled.

"I think he figured you were going to haul his ass off to jail."

"Yeah, the way he jackrabbited out of here, I think you're right. Now let's get to work."

Oil and grease stains covered the carpeting. Obviously, the living room was the area where Carole worked on her motorcycle. In the far corner, stacks of flattened cardboard boxes were also stained with grease, but they obviously hadn't been enough to absorb whatever procedure Carole had performed in her living room. The tool chest was packed with an assortment of tools that would have made any mechanic drool.

The stains carried over into the kitchen, where the counters and porcelain sink were smudged and stained from someone's greasy hands.

The back of the house looked more clean and livable. The double bed was made and the bathroom was spotless. Carole's bedspread depicted a couple riding a motorcycle along the ocean, their hair flying wildly behind them. The only picture hanging in the apartment was a poster over the bed. That too was a motorcycle rider, but this one was of a woman riding nude on a Harley.

"Tastefully done," Scott commented.

"Oh, I didn't know you were a Harley buff," Gwen teased.

"I mean, the way the woman in the picture is photographed. It's a sexy…uh, not a vulgar photograph," Scott said tactfully, obviously uncomfortable discussing it with Gwen.

"Yeah. I kinda like it too. Hey, here's a laptop," she said, pulling open the nightstand drawer. She slid it into an evidence bag to take back with her.

The two were silent as they riffled through the rest of the drawers, finding nothing else of significance.

"I'll let the crime scene crew know we're through here so they can come over when they're finished at Amy's," Scott said.

As he finished the call there was a knock on the door and Brad and CC tiptoed in.

"You guys finished both places already?" Brad asked.

"If you'd have seen Amy's place, you'd know why we're done here already. There was nothing…I mean nada…except a mattress and a couple of empty boxes," Scott informed them.

CC slipped into paper slippers and walked toward the living room. "How gross! This place is a mess."

Gwen told them about catching Thomas Planton stealing the tools, and they joked about scaring the kid half to death.

"Looks like Carole brought her Harley into the living room with her at night. The back is more presentable," Gwen told them. "Find anything at Meg's?"

"Yeah. We found a computer and nosed around her Facebook page. She complained about someone following her and being a bully. No names, but she referred to him as someone in authority," Brad advised.

Gwen groaned. "You mean like one of us? A cop?"

"Not again!" Scott frowned.

"She doesn't say specifically," CC added. "Could be anybody with authority at this point...teacher, executive, boss...who knows. We bagged it and tagged it."

"Got an address book too," Brad remembered. "The woman was popular. It's got to have a hundred names in it. Thought I'd take it back to the precinct and have a couple uniforms get started on it."

"Good idea," Gwen said thoughtfully. "It's getting late. Anyone want a burger before we head out to The Dive? It's on me."

They all murmured their agreement, and headed out.

CHAPTER TWENTY

A Burger King was right around the corner. Sitting at a table next to the window, the four cops enjoyed themselves, joking and ribbing each other throughout dinner.

"You've got ketchup smeared all over your cheek," she told CC, wondering what the men would do if she leapt over the table to lick it off.

"I do enjoy my food, even if it doesn't all end up in the right place," CC said good-naturedly, wiping her face with her napkin. "My mom always made me wear an old shirt when we went out to eat, 'cause inevitably I'd end up with something spilled on the front of me."

Scott said, "I had a first date with this gal I really liked. Well, halfway through dinner she excuses herself and runs to the restroom. She just bolted from the table and ran down the hall to the john. So, I'm sitting there waiting, and waiting, and waiting. About forty-five minutes later, after I'd finished my meal, I asked the waitress to go into the restroom to see if she was all right. Turns out she had the flu and got sick all over herself. She was too embarrassed to come back to the table, so she hailed a cab and went home."

"You waited forty-five minutes to have someone check on her?" Gwen joked.

"Man, I'll never forget that porterhouse," Scott smirked. "When she didn't return, I started in on her shrimp. Hey, I was gonna have to pay for it whether she returned or not!"

"What about you, Gwen. Do you have a most embarrassing date?" CC asked.

"Hmm…I had a date get sick on the Ferris wheel at the state fair, but she was very neat about it…barfed into her purse. And I took her home afterward, not like some people," she kidded Scott.

They all groaned. "It's almost seven thirty. I suppose we should get going. Gwen stood and stretched. "Brad, can you take the laptop we found at Carole's back to the precinct?"

"Sure. No problem."

"They should have Meg's tower there by now. I'd like to see if you can find any similarities…chat rooms, friends, or acquaintances. And try to get more info on who Meg thought was following her."

"I'm on it," Brad said, getting up from the table. "I'll see if Charlie's available. I'd like to walk the area around The Dive again later too."

"I'm heading out," Scott told them. "I want to be in place before you two women arrive."

When Gwen and CC were alone, Gwen said, "I miss you!"

"I miss you too," CC admitted. "How long do you think we'll have to hang around The Dive tonight?"

"Seems like the majority of the action is between nine and eleven. Midnight tops."

"That's reasonable. Your place or mine? And I promise not to fall asleep on you tonight," CC said.

"I'll stick around again until after you're out safely, so if you don't mind, let's make it your place. God, I can't wait to be with you again," Gwen said huskily. "I'll be out the door fifteen minutes after you leave."

***

The Dive filled up as quickly as it had the previous evening. Many of the same regulars greeted Gwen as she sat down at the bar. She noticed CC starting a pool game with one of the men in the back. From time to time, she glanced over to see CC winning by a good margin. She was good at the game, and Gwen had all she could do to keep from watching CC's sexy ass as she leaned over the table to make a shot. A couple she hadn't seen before entered and sat on the two stools to her right. They introduced themselves as Jeff and Jackie.

Jeff was short, barely five foot, with tattoos of snakes winding up his arms and into his neck. His swarthy face was pockmarked. He looked to be at least a hundred pounds overweight. At his side, Jackie was thin, and towered over him by a foot. She had long, stringy, bleached blond hair. They wore matching leather jackets and jeans.

"Sure is a bummer about those girls," Jeff said after they'd been chatting a while.

"Yeah, aren't you afraid of being here alone?" Jackie asked Gwen.

"Nah, I've taken karate," Gwen said lightly. "Besides, the men have taken their responsibility seriously to walk all the single women to their cars."

"Still, I'm glad I have Jeff with me." Jackie smiled and leaned over to kiss her boyfriend.

"Did you know any of the women?" Gwen asked.

"Everyone knew Meg," Jackie answered. "She was the first to disappear. I thought she was being paranoid, but she told me one night that a cop was bugging her. I didn't know the other two that well." She nervously chewed off some of the polish on her short nails.

"No kidding, a cop?" Gwen did not have to feign her surprise.

"Yeah. She said she thought he just wanted to get in her pants. He was always following her and when she'd get home, she'd see him sitting in his car watching her apartment." Jackie shook her head, her face reddening with disgust at the thought of it.

"Did you tell this to any of the police investigating the disappearances?" Gwen asked.

"No, we were out of town visiting my parents during the week Ben said they'd been interviewing everyone. Guess I should report it, huh?"

Gwen took a deep breath, trying not to strangle this woman. "Might be important," she finally said. "I would definitely give them a call."

"I'll do it tomorrow, promise," Jackie said thoughtfully.

"Did Meg say what the guy looked like? I mean, if we know who to look out for, the rest of us may be able to avoid getting in trouble," Gwen prodded.

"Just that he was an old guy. You know, tough-looking with a grayish brush haircut," Jackie told her. "She didn't say much. For as tiny as she was, Meg was all bravado, wasn't she Jeff?"

"Yeah, she was a little black spitfire, for sure," Jeff agreed. "Played a hell of a game of darts, and I could never figure out how she was able to make all those terrific pool shots, being that her reach was so short. Beat me every game and whipped most of the other guys too."

Jeff started talking to Jackie about not wanting to make another trip to her parents' place in northern Wisconsin, so Gwen turned her attention back to the rest of the group at the bar. Everyone was still speculating about the missing women, and Gwen caught snippets of conversation about different theories they'd come up with. She noticed CC had finished playing pool and was sitting at a table talking with the woman she'd met the previous evening. Thinking back to her report, Gwen remembered that the woman's name was Reyna. They were deep in conversation.

"You look distracted tonight." Ben had walked up and was studying her. "Dart league practices Wednesdays and Fridays, but Jimmy wants to know if you'll play a game with him and give him a few pointers. He's too shy to ask you himself."

"Sure," Gwen laughed. "Tell him I'd be happy to."

As they were finishing up their third game, Gwen noticed CC leaving. It was ten minutes before midnight.

"That's it for me," Gwen said after letting Jimmy win the last game. "Work on that curve and try to straighten it out. You could be a great player with a little more practice."

"You really think so?" Jimmy asked with a silly grin.

"Of course. Practice makes perfect."

Gwen walked back, said her goodbyes, threw a tip on the bar and headed out the door.

"Hold on, young lady." Jimmy ran up to her and gallantly escorted her to her car.

CHAPTER TWENTY-ONE

Gwen arrived at CC's just before 12:30 a.m. She was waiting at the door barefoot, in a silk, midnight-blue robe. Gwen took her hand and gaped at the plunging neckline and her long, slender legs. Her blond hair was still damp, hanging in golden waves down to her shoulders.

"You look fantastic," she finally said.

"You don't look so bad yourself," CC said, tugging at Gwen's jacket as she was slipping out of it.

They walked hand in hand to the living room where CC's stereo was playing softly in the background.

"Can I have this dance?" Gwen asked, putting her arms around CC. They moved close together, holding each other affectionately, their feet barely moving as they swayed to the music.

"I've been waiting for this all day," CC whispered in Gwen's ear.

"I've been waiting for you for a lifetime," Gwen responded, sliding her hand under CC's robe to feel her taut breasts. She could smell the faint scent of lilacs as she nuzzled CC, kissing her neck gently and lightly nibbling her earlobes.

When she could wait no longer, Gwen kissed CC urgently, her tongue darting between CC's velvety lips in swift thrusts. Her hand moved down CC's stomach until she reached her thighs. CC opened her legs, welcoming Gwen's touch.

Her crotch was warm and wet, and CC cried out as Gwen stroked her clit, "Hurry!"

Gwen smiled wickedly and whispered, "No, I want to tease you."

Gwen knelt down and unfastened the tie around CC's waist. CC quickly slid out of the robe, letting it fall to the floor.

Gwen's tongue started stroking slowly between CC's upper thighs, belly and back again. She savored the firm swelling of CC's clit, then circled her crotch with her tongue and nibbled at her skin until CC moaned with desire. When she finally thrust her fingers into CC's welcoming vagina, CC tensed, quivered and exploded, shuddering with pleasure.

Gwen stood and kissed CC passionately.

"My God, that was fantastic." CC sighed. "You take my breath away."

"And my heart dances with delight at the taste and feel of you. I think I will never get enough," Gwen said softly.

"Let's go into the bedroom," CC said, leading the way. "My turn."

Gwen slipped out of her clothes and laid next to CC, overcome with desire for her tender touch. The throbbing between her legs made her feel ready to explode.

CC wasted no time covering Gwen's body with tiny butterfly kisses and gently probing with her fingers. Moments later, Gwen's body shook and she screamed in delight.

"I'm not a bit tired yet, are you?" CC smiled, propping herself up on one elbow.

Gwen smiled mischievously. "Not at all."

They took turns pleasuring each other until they finally lay exhausted. CC turned to her side and Gwen pressed her body close as they slept in a tight cocoon, content and completely satisfied.

***

Gwen awoke at nine a.m. and eased herself out of bed. She tiptoed to the bathroom and turned on the shower until the steam was fogging the mirrors. She'd just slipped under the tepid stream when CC slipped in beside her. They washed each other and played, enjoying each other's bodies and bringing each other to another orgasm before stepping out.

"What a way to wake up," CC laughed, rubbing her towel briskly over her skin.

"Umm, I could get used to this." Gwen smiled and gave CC a quick, fervent kiss.

Gwen kissed CC again and reluctantly took off to go home, change clothes, and get ready for their meeting.

CHAPTER TWENTY-TWO

Brad was excited to tell everyone that they had found a ton of Facebook chatter on both Carole's laptop and Meg's PC.

"We don't have a name, but we're still looking. He is a big man, older…short gray hair. Wears a uniform," Brad told them as soon as the task force meeting started.

Gwen nodded. "That confirms what we've learned from some of the people at the bar."

"Meg wrote one of her friends that this man had followed her home several times. She'd lock and chain her door behind her, but said 'it was creepy looking out the window seeing him stare at my place. I think he's too old to be a threat. I will find out soon what he's up to'," Brad read from his notes.

"Gives me the creeps just hearing her words."

"I talked to Carole's mom…uh, Pauline Planton. She told about the same story. Carole said some old man was following her and she was getting ready to beat the crap out of him if it continued," Scott added. "Carole told her mom not to worry, that she always hung around where there were a lot of other people. If she was worried, she made light of it when talking with her family."

"She had three grown brothers, so I'd imagine she could have enlisted their help if she thought the man was dangerous," Gwen mused.

"So the perp isn't hiding his presence from the women. He lets them see him watch them. They think he's harmless because he's an older man, but they're all curious to talk to him and find out why they're so interesting to him," CC pondered. "I wonder if the uniform is real or a disguise."

"Interesting question. Does either describe the car he drives?" Gwen asked.

"Meg mentioned a black sedan," Brad answered, "but that could describe any of a number of makes and models. We don't know if it's new or old."

"I'll check out any black cars more carefully at The Dive tonight," Scott offered. "At least that's something."

"I'm still canvassing the area," Brad told them. "There's a lot of real estate to cover, but my circle is widening. I've walked the block where The Dive is located, and I'll be starting the next blocks surrounding it tonight."

"Oh, and a Jackie something-or-other called to let us know Meg told her she was being followed by a cop," Scott remembered.

"About damn time she made the call," Gwen remarked. "She and her boyfriend were out of town when the bar's staff and customers were being interviewed. I suggested last night that she call and report the conversation. Give her a call back, Scott, see if she remembers anything else. Bring her in if you think she's holding anything back."

"Will do."

"Let's head out."

***

The Dive was quiet tonight, with only a half dozen people at the bar and eight people playing pool. Reyna, of course, was close to the pool tables, taking in the action and making small talk with everyone who stopped at her table.

Since no one was playing darts tonight, Gwen ordered a beer and carried it to the back room. She plopped her quarters down at the edge of the pool table and waited her turn, sitting with Reyna and CC, who had just returned from the ladies' room.

After Gwen introduced herself to Reyna and CC, Reyna immediately went into her routine to find out as much as possible about the new woman.

"What brings you here?" she inquired.

"I like the games, and the people here are awfully friendly," Gwen replied.

"You been in Scarletsville long?"

"Long enough, I guess," Gwen answered vaguely.

"Whatcha do for a living?" Reyna probed.

"Nothing right now," Gwen countered. "I inherited a little dough awhile back."

"Betcha my youngest would take hell of a liking to a lady like yourself." Reyna grinned.

"Ah, sorry to disappoint you, but I'm gay."

"Even better. He enjoys a happy woman," Reyna said innocently.

Gwen winked at CC and said, "I mean, I like women, not men."

"Oh my, Lordy!" Reyna exclaimed, and for the first time was at a loss for words.

CC looked at Gwen and they both burst out laughing. Reyna soon joined in, forgetting her blunder. She ordered one of the men to get them a round of drinks, just as it was Gwen's turn to play.

Gwen picked CC to be her partner against the two men who had just won the last game. Gwen broke the rack of balls and had sunk two in succession when they heard commotion at the bar, then sirens coming closer and people were getting up to go outside to see what was happening.

Gwen whispered to CC, "Let's see what's going on." As they headed out, the rest of the pool players followed, leaving a frustrated Reyna behind fiddling with the controls of her motorized scooter.

"They caught the guy who took the women!" someone yelled.

They ran to the back of the parking lot where they saw Brad with his knee on the back of a husky, squirming, dark-haired young man, roughly cuffing his hands behind his back. A half dozen uniformed cops jumped from their squads and rushed forward to help. Brad pulled a plastic zip tie from his pocket and wrapped it around the young man's ankles, then forcefully pulled him to his feet.

"I haven't done anything wrong!" the young man cried out.

"Then why were you running?" Brad asked.

"You scared the shit out of me!" he spat. "I didn't know anyone else was out here. Oh, crap! I got scared."

"What are you doing sneaking around out here?" Brad demanded.

"I'm looking for my sister. Carole. She disappeared a couple days ago. Thought I could try to find her," the man said defiantly.

"You got ID on you?" one of the uniformed officers asked.

"In my back pocket."

The cop pulled a greasy-looking wallet from the boy's pocket and flipped it open. "Carl Planton," he read.

Gwen realized he was the brother of Thomas Planton, who they'd found at Carole's apartment.

"Geez," Brad muttered under his breath, then to Carl, "Let the police handle it. Go home and I don't want to catch you out here again, you hear?"

"Yeah. Just let me go."

Brad cut the tie from around the kid's ankles and opened the cuffs. Carl massaged his wrists and looked around, noticing for the first time the crowd that had gathered. He turned crimson and took off running in the opposite direction.

Not wanting to blow their cover, CC and Gwen followed the crowd back into The Dive and resumed their pool game.

Around eleven thirty, Gwen noticed CC yawning and nodded knowingly, letting her know it was okay to leave. It was doubtful there would be any more action tonight. One of the men they were playing pool with escorted her to her car. Gwen ordered another beer and played for another hour. She wasn't in a hurry to go home to her empty house.

CHAPTER TWENTY-THREE

Gwen took the stairs one floor up to her office. She was pleasantly surprised to see CC sitting at the spare desk looking over some files.

"Hey there," Gwen said cheerily. "How's it going?"

"Pretty well, actually. I slept like a baby last night, and started early. I stopped by the Planton residence and was able to talk to the whole crew…Carl, Tom and Billy were all there, as well as the mother, Pauline."

"Good thinking," Gwen said thoughtfully.

"Billy is the only one with a record. He was heavily into car theft with his friends during his senior year of high school. He's twenty now, seems to be settling down…says he has a serious girlfriend and wants to get married and have a family. He's been holding down a steady job at Paradise Auto for about six months. Carl, the boy Brad tagged last night, is nineteen. He's still rebellious, but doesn't get into too much trouble according to his mother. He spends most of his time in his room playing computer games or downtown at the video arcade."

She looked at her notes. "The third boy, Tom, is the youngest—eighteen. He's the one you caught stealing tools at Carole's. He has a bit of an attitude, but I don't think we'll have any more trouble with him. I read them all the riot act and scolded them about interfering with our investigation. I have a feeling they understood what I was going to do with them if I caught them again, with even the slightest infraction."

Gwen laughed. "You are tough! But thanks. I think it was a great idea to speak with them and give them all a warning about getting in our way again. I had nightmares that we rushed out of The Dive and blew our cover. Had Brad not already had the situation under control, we might have had to step in."

"I'll take that as a compliment." Brad smiled, stepping into the office holding a box of Krispy Kreme doughnuts.

"Of course." Gwen laughed. "And you're buttering us up too?" she said, peering into the box and grabbing a glazed doughnut.

"Thought we could all use a little treat."

"If it's a bribe, I'm not eating," Scott said, coming in behind Brad.

"Whatever do you mean, good buddy?" Brad asked in feigned surprise.

"That caramel latte you bought for me yesterday was no way enough payment for those horrible follow-up calls I made for you. Three out of the six were screamers," Scott complained.

"Hey, I thought they'd be easy. Sorry, guy. I just didn't want you thinking you were being left out while I was downloading information from the girls' PCs," Brad said innocently.

"Yeah, right!" Scott huffed, and dug into the box of doughnuts. "Better be watching your back, buddy." He smiled good-naturedly.

"You two!" Gwen laughed. "Let's get back to work."

"I've almost finished checking out the staff and customers at The Dive," Scott volunteered. "Other than the couple being iffy and us putting a tag on them, everyone seems legit."

"Which couple?" CC asked.

"Oh, sorry," Scott apologized. "Jackie and Jeff. They're people Gwen ran into at the bar, and they're either very nosy or know something they shouldn't. I've got someone following them for a few days."

"Still checking out the neighborhood. I didn't get very far last night because of all the bullshit," Brad admitted. "Damn, I was so hoping I'd tackled the perp."

"How bad is the backup of callbacks from the hotline?" Gwen asked Brad.

"I'd say there are at least a couple dozen that should be followed up on. All I've had time to do is screen them, and discard the crank calls and those I'm sure aren't significant to the investigation."

"CC, if you don't mind, you and I will stay here tonight and get those caught up. Scott, you can continue your surveillance from the parking lot to make sure no one else disappears, and Brad, that will give you more time to scour the neighborhood."

"I don't mind at all," CC replied. "I think it's a good idea to mix it up a little. People might get suspicious if we're hanging around too much."

"Okay, it's a done deal. Let's get 'em," Gwen said cheerfully.

Gwen and CC split up the calls and got started as soon as Brad and Scott left the office. Most of the time, in Gwen's experience, people phoned into a hotline out of panic and changed their minds when an officer returned their call; it was difficult to come up with a substantial complaint when it was only a nagging fear that spurred them to make the call in the first place. Often they called to get someone they were angry with in trouble, and ended up recanting their accusations when their anger had a chance to simmer down. Very few calls resulted in capturing the perp they were looking for, and a good detective could weed out the crazies and liars quickly and immediately get someone to investigate the few legitimate tips that might lead to an arrest.

Within three hours, the two women finished the stack of messages Brad had left for them. Gwen went down to the call center and picked up a new stack of about a dozen messages and brought steaming cups of coffee back with her.

"Smells good. Thanks!" CC smiled. "You read my mind."

"I figured we could take a break before we start in again. My back is killing me from sitting in one spot for so long," Gwen complained.

Just as Gwen took her first sip of coffee, her cell phone rang. It was Brad.

"I found a body," he said grimly. "It's about three blocks from the bar, hidden behind some bushes in an empty field. Thought you might want to take a look. I think it's Carole Planton."

"God. Okay, we'll be there as soon as possible," Gwen told him.

"What's wrong?" CC asked, seeing the concern on Gwen's face and knowing the news couldn't be good.

"Brad found one of the women. Possibly Carole," Gwen replied. "Let's go."

They made it to the overgrown field in about twenty minutes.

It was cold and dark, but crime scene technicians were already stringing lights around the bare tree limbs and setting up spotlights on poles, making the scene look like a surreal Christmas display. The woman lay on her back, with her head tilted slightly to the right and her knees bent away from the bushes. Her eyes were frozen open with a look of sheer terror, and blood was caked into the folds of her neck. The front of a white T-shirt was stained crimson, like someone had tie-dyed a grotesque splotch onto the neckline and another around the stomach. She was fully clothed, but wasn't wearing a jacket. Her hands were clenched at her sides into the leaves and soil. Carefully, with one gloved finger, one of the techs lifted the T-shirt to reveal a knife wound to her belly. The intestines were spilling out of the three-inch gash, most likely resulting when the knife was withdrawn.

"There's too much dried blood to be certain," Brad spoke quietly, "but looks like the wound to her neck extends from ear to ear. Not deep enough to decapitate her, but clearly enough for her to bleed out. The stab wound to her abdomen was overkill. We found no purse, no ID. But it looks like Carole."

"Looks like he had a hell of a lot of pent-up anger against his victim," Gwen observed. "It doesn't look like he picked her at random. He had a score to settle."

"The only tie-in we've come up with among the three was The Dive. Maybe we should take a closer look at the people there," CC said to no one in particular, staring off into the distance.

"Hey, Brad, that reminds me. How far did you get with the address book you found at Meg's?" Gwen asked.

Standing up, he scratched his head. "Shit. I've been so busy I forgot all about it. It's in my desk drawer. Sorry."

"Don't worry about it. We'll take a look when we get back," Gwen said just as the coroner, Doc Maynard, walked up to her.

"My dear Gwen. I didn't think I'd be seeing you so soon again."

"Neither did I, Doc. It's always a pleasure though," she said kindly.

"What do we have here?" he said, crouching beside the corpse with reverent interest, unlike the disrespectful mannerisms of some of the officers. He put his case down, snapped on a pair of gloves.

"Any idea how long she's been out here?" Gwen asked.

"Hard to say." He picked up a hand, pulled at the skin; it was loose. "With this weather, close to freezing at night and sunny during the day, would be difficult to say with certainty. My guess is three, maybe four days max."

He gently moved the woman's head from side to side and then eased the T-shirt up to examine the stab wound to her torso. "Died from the cut to her throat. The cut to her abdomen, although it looks bad, wouldn't have killed her quickly."

He pulled glasses out of his breast pocket, and scrutinized the wound more carefully. "Ahh…it was inflicted postmortem. Appears to be lacerated with a butcher knife…something with a long, wide blade. Hmm…that's interesting."

He got up and crouched behind the woman's head, and leaned over her body, waving his hand over her belly. "See here?

The cut is moving up toward her head and not down as it is most often with this kind of wound. He stabbed her from this angle."

"What does that mean?" CC asked, confused.

"Might have been planning on making the mark of a cross, but the knife hit the breastbone and he couldn't cut through the hard tissue." He lifted the blouse further to reveal her upper chest. "Yup, see this faint line dissecting the throat? I'll know more when I perform the autopsy."

"When do you think you can do it?" Gwen asked anxiously.

"First thing tomorrow. See you at six a.m. sharp?"

Gwen groaned, and then replied, "I'll be there. Anything more you can tell me now, Doc?"

"No. We'll get her fingerprinted and I want her clothes vacuumed before I move her. They'll scour the area and I'll advise you immediately if anything turns up. See you in the morning."

Gwen and CC returned to the precinct, leaving the crime scene technicians to process the area and the coroner's people to remove the body. In the squad room, they reviewed the pictures of the three missing women which were taped next to the white board listing the evidence they'd found so far, as well as other information they thought might be pertinent.

"It's Carole," CC said softly, staring at the pictures in front of her.

"No doubt about it."

"I'll do the notify if you'd like. I don't mind," CC offered.

"Thanks. That would be great. Do you want to attend the autopsy?" Gwen asked.

"If you don't mind…uh, I'll pass. It's not that I'm squeamish, but if I have a choice…uh, and you'll be there…and after talking to the family, I feel like I knew her…" CC stammered.

"It's okay." Gwen smiled understandingly. "I'll call you." She was just about to grab CC and give her a reassuring hug when Brad walked in.

"Here's the address book from Meg's apartment," he said, handing it to Gwen.

"Great. I just want to page through it before I leave. Maybe you and CC can work on it more thoroughly in the morning.

After the autopsy I have a bail hearing to attend. Captain Wright's lawyers are trying to get him out on bail."

"You've got to be kidding me," Brad said angrily. "The son of a bitch killed two people and nearly slaughtered a third!"

"Innocent until proven guilty," Gwen said firmly. "I think we have enough evidence to convince the judge to deny bail. The chief did some personal legwork and found out that Wright has some interesting connections, as well as prime real estate in Florida. We believe he'd bolt out of state if not the country in a flash if he was freed."

"What kind of connections?" CC asked.

"Several phone calls on his office phone were placed to the Wisconsin State Prison. Chief Ziegler put an investigator on it. One of the jail snitches accused Wright of being on the take for a smuggling mob based out of Tampa. Seems he bungled a couple of investigations having to do with some stolen jewelry and expensive paintings. Mostly we have him nailed on the murders. When his house was searched, we found the boots with the tiny crack in the sole, and the jacket with the square of fabric missing which is an exact match to the swatch CC found on the snowmobile trail. All the evidence leads directly to him."

"His kind reflects on the entire force," Brad exploded. "I hope he gets a needle in his arm."

"The picture we're painting of Wright just keeps getting better and better," CC said facetiously.

"Like I said, I don't think he'll be freed. We'll nail him to the cross at trial," Gwen assured them.

"I sure hope you're right." CC sighed.

"Hey, look at this," Gwen said, paging through Meg's address book. "Kathy Wright's name is here. I didn't know they were friends."

"No kidding?" CC asked in surprise. "That's odd."

"I didn't find any chitchat between the two of them on Facebook, but I did find some odd e-mails where I hadn't been able to identify the source. Anyone know what Kathy's e-mail address was?" Brad asked.

"I seem to remember years ago it was something like 'Katydid'," Gwen replied.

"That could be it. I'll go back and print them out," Brad said, hurrying off.

"I wonder if Carole or Amy are in here," Gwen mumbled, paging through the book. "Hmm...there's a CP...could be Carole. And an Amie with no last name...she could have spelled Amy wrong."

"I'll leave this with you, CC," Gwen said, turning the book over to her. "See if you can find someone who will talk to you who might know the relationships between the missing girls. Have a photo spread made up with Kathy and the three from The Dive. Throw in a couple of other mugshots and see if anyone listed in that book can connect the dots for us."

"I'm on it," CC answered.

CHAPTER TWENTY-FOUR

When her alarm went off at four a.m, Gwen was jarred out of a deep sleep.

"I am so not ready to get up," she mumbled, and hit the snooze button to give herself another ten minutes. She had fallen asleep again when the alarm sounded once more. She nearly tripped on Max as she got out of bed. Pierre must be out of town, she thought, making a mental note to pick up dog biscuits and dog food on the way home.

She put on her sweats and began her exercise routine. As her head cleared from the fog of slumber, she mentally reviewed her morning. First was the autopsy, which shouldn't last more than an hour. She then rehearsed the argument she planned to give at Wright's bail hearing.

She grabbed Max's leash and ran around the block with him until he'd finished his business. A half hour later she took a long, brisk shower, dressed in her navy pants suit with a baby blue turtleneck underneath, and made a cup of black coffee to take with her.

***

"Very good. You're right on time," Doc said cheerfully as Gwen stepped into the morgue.

"I don't know how people can be so happy at this time of the morning," she grumbled in response.

He laughed. "At my age, waking up to a new day is a big deal. Of course, I've always been a morning person. It's the best time of the day."

"So they say," Gwen huffed.

"Ready to get started?" Doc asked.

"Sure," Gwen said, drinking the last dregs of her coffee and throwing the Styrofoam cup into the garbage. She donned a paper gown and smeared mentholated salve under her nose to mask the smell of decomposition that permeated the room.

"Unremarkable body structure," Doc Maynard started dictating into the mouthpiece extending downward from his right ear. "Victim is sixty-five inches tall, weight is one hundred thirty-two pounds. Light brown hair, length just below her earlobes. Clothes transported with body: white T-shirt, black slacks, white socks, beige sports bra and white Reebok tennis shoes. Packaged and sent to lab for trace. Taking nail scrapings now…seems to be a substantial amount of soil and debris from the area where the body was discovered. Make a note with a marker if you will, Gwen, on this plastic sack, 'Compare to soil samples taken at site.'"

He continued, "Seems to be a fair amount of soil contaminating the dried blood. Let's see how much of it we can save." He expertly scraped the dried blood around her neck into another plastic bag.

After meticulously cleaning the skin around her neck and torso, Doc continued, "Incision extends from ear to ear on front side of neck, approximately six and three-quarters inches long, two inches deep. Smooth cut; no jagged edges. Severed jugular vein just below collarbone. Extensive bleeding into esophageal cavity."

Moving to the midsection he continued taking measurements. "Stab wound four and one half inches below breastbone is three inches wide, two and one half inches deep. Smooth cut; no jagged edges. Rapid withdrawal of cutting instrument tore upper intestine. Knife continues to a lesser depth, barely breaking skin upward to a point just past throat incision. Ready to check body cavities."

He took a small circular saw and expertly cut the crown of the skull and weighed the brain at 1327 grams, dictating his findings into the tape recorder. He then made an incision along the woman's torso, being careful not to disturb the wounds. He weighed her lungs, heart and kidneys and took samples of her stomach contents. "She hadn't eaten for several hours," Doc explained his results as he moved along. "Didn't go down easily though. She was a fighter and was possibly thrown to the ground during the struggle. See this dark material in her stomach? It's the probably the same soil as we found under her fingernails. We can test it to see if it matches the soil where she was found. There could have been an altercation before he started cutting her."

"Think we'll find scratch marks on the guy who attacked her?" Gwen asked.

"Don't know. He may have worn a layer of protective clothing …possibly even gloves. Unfortunately, although I've seen a few fibers, nothing I'd recognize as skin tissue. Of course, that's for the lab to confirm. I've been surprised more than once by what they've come up with which was invisible to the naked eye."

When he finished his examination, he carefully started sewing shut the layers of flesh he'd opened. "I've put a rush on the findings. Hope to get back with you soon," he told Gwen.

"I appreciate that, Doc. Thanks," Gwen said, shedding her protective gear and hurrying out of the morgue.

The courthouse was only two blocks away, but Gwen decided to park in her assigned spot at the precinct where she'd only have to walk across the street. It was already seven thirty, so she had to hurry.

As she crossed the parking lot, CC was coming out of the Administrative Building and heading to her car.

"Wow," she whistled when she caught up to Gwen. "I've never seen you so dressed up."

"Well, I can look presentable if I have to," Gwen said, blushing.

"You look great! You have a few minutes?"

"I've got to be at Wright's hearing in a half hour. I'm on my way now," Gwen said.

"Mind if I walk with you?"

"Hell no! What did you do, sleep at your desk?" Gwen kidded.

"No, but I couldn't sleep, so I got here early again. I've already made a couple calls…not making any points waking people up at seven a.m., but I found someone who knew Meg really well. Said she might have met Kathy a couple times at Meg's place. She agreed to meet with me if I bought breakfast. And I already have the photo layout. The guys were nice enough to work on it last night." CC beamed, showing Gwen the sheet with six women's photographs.

"Yeah, they did a good job," she agreed as they reached the courtroom door. "Well, I'd better go in. Good luck and be careful."

"You too!"

CHAPTER TWENTY-FIVE

The courtroom was packed to overflowing. TV cameras were positioned in a cramped space in the back and reporters, family, friends and the curious filled every available seat not reserved for the defense and prosecution.

As everyone was taking their places, Gwen noticed Captain Wright walk in stiffly with his lawyer. He was wearing a blue suit, white shirt and red and blue tie. He had a smug expression on his face and carried himself with an air of authority, like he was going to a business meeting instead of a court hearing. He wasn't cuffed, but two well-armed guards stood close by. His lawyer was a small man, but had a crooked grin and a dishonest look about him. From the rumors Gwen had heard, Jordan Bell was an expert at defending scumbags like Wright, and had an excellent record of successes.

Gwen waved to the district attorney assigned to the case, Sydney Fellerman. She had worked with him on many other occasions, and found the man to be brilliant, dedicated and honest. He was tall and athletic, and known to spend his spare time running marathons.

"All rise," the bailiff announced, and Judge John Garmer stepped to the bench. Garmer was the last jurist Gwen would have picked had she had a choice in the matter. He was known for his insensitivity and quick decisions, allowing only brief sidebars between the lawyers. Once his mind was made up, it was not easily swayed, no matter how complicated the legal interpretation that the lawyers were arguing. Rumor had it he was close to retiring, and Gwen now wished he had already made that a reality.

Fellerman summarized the charges against Wright and made it clear that he was a flight risk. He didn't go as far as accusing the man of having ties to the mob, but made it known that some of his associates were shady and not always law abiding. He tactfully outlined the State's contention that Wright should not be set free until his trial under any circumstances. Garmer refused Fellerman's request to submit further evidence substantiating Wright's crimes and present witnesses.

Bell was quick to dispute the evidence Fellerman had presented as purely circumstantial, and made Wright sound like an innocent choirboy. He extolled his achievements on the police force and named numerous committees he had headed on behalf of the State. Another list of his volunteer work and donations depicted Wright as a man who kept nothing for himself, but gave most of his time and money to the needy.

Gwen wanted to throw up, and felt the bile rising in her throat. She got more and more angry and disgusted as Bell's description of this killer continued. Finally, he sat down and the judge called a fifteen-minute recess.

Fellerman turned back and looked at Gwen, a helpless frown plastered on his face. He shrugged and turned back to face the front of the courtroom.

When the judge returned, he quickly recited his verdict. "Bail granted pending payment of a two hundred thousand dollar bond."

Gwen nearly cried. For a mere twenty thousand, Wright would be able to purchase his freedom. He would only need to put up ten percent in cash. Wright smiled broadly and shook his lawyer's hand.

When she shuffled out of the courtroom with the rest of the crowd, Fellerman caught up to her and whispered, "We'll get him at trial. I promise."

Gwen could only nod, wracked with fear she'd lose her composure if she spoke.

***

Back at the precinct she met with Brad and Scott and brought them up to date with the judge's decision. CC hadn't returned from her interview. She also informed Scott about the possible connection between Meg and Kathy.

"I almost wish the captain does hightail it out of here and head for Florida. At least then he won't be underfoot," Scott commented.

"I can't believe he'd stick around. With the murder charges pending against him and the wealth of information backing up the fact that he was into some underhanded dealings, not to mention using his position to his own advantage, he'll never get another job on the force...or for the city for that matter," Brad added.

Gwen shook her head. "Leaving will make him look guilty, and from the smug satisfaction he displayed in the courtroom this morning, I'm sure he expects to be fully exonerated. He doesn't appear to have a worry in the world."

"What's going on?" CC popped her head in. "What'd I miss?"

"Wright's out on bail," Brad said miserably.

"What? That's incredible." Then turning to Gwen, "I'm so sorry. You were so sure."

"Yeah, we'll just have to deal with it. Scott, do you know anyone we can have tail Wright who he won't recognize?"

"There's a real green recruit he couldn't possibly pick out. The kid's been out of the academy for only three weeks, and he seems like a real go-getter."

"Perfect. I'll request to have him transferred. He'll be assigned to you so you can keep tabs on him. Okay, Scott?" Gwen asked.

"Sure. I don't mind giving the kid a few pointers," Scott said, lifting his arms with his elbows pointing out, pretending to groom his own feathers.

"You come up with anything?" Gwen asked CC, laughing and dismissing Scott's antics.

"Yeah. Meg and Kathy met frequently at some bar. Meg's friend didn't know which one, but she was sure it wasn't The Dive. Toward the end, Linda met the two a couple times at Meg's apartment. They wanted her to join them in a business venture. Linda was reluctant because it would wipe out her savings, but they had a good idea about recycling used clothing, and offering office women on a low budget nice outfits for dirt cheap prices. Meg was a whiz at putting clothing and accessories together in an attractive way, and Kathy had no shame when it came to searching bargain stores or riffling through neighborhood donation boxes. Linda did freelance marketing and artwork, so they wanted her to make flyers and pay for some advertising in exchange for a percentage of the profits."

"Okay, the story sounds logical. Sure wish we knew where Meg and Kathy met for their little powwows though," Gwen said thoughtfully.

"Linda doesn't drink, so she always met with them at Meg's place. I'll tell you one thing though, Linda is freaked out that Kathy is dead and Meg is missing. She's very much afraid."

"Has she seen anyone following her?" Brad asked, concerned.

"No. She has nothing to substantiate her fears. No strange cars or men hanging around. She has my card. I made sure she understood she could call me twenty-four/seven if she thought of anything else, or noticed something suspicious going on."

"Okay. It's been a long morning. I'm going home to try to get some rest before we meet at The Dive tonight. I suggest you all do the same," Gwen told them.

They all looked beat. Gwen was sure no one would refuse her offer for a few free hours to get refreshed before another long night.

CHAPTER TWENTY-SIX

Gwen awoke in a tangle of covers, bathed in sweat. Captain Wright, a wicked snarl on his lips, had held his hand around her neck. The other hand held a knife that was inches from her heart, ready to slice into her flesh.

She had an eerie feeling about the captain running around as a free man. Nothing would surprise her about the evil man.

She glanced at the clock. Six ten p.m. She had slept four hours, and she still had plenty of time before she needed to be at The Dive. It would be nice to pamper herself with a nice hot bubble bath before getting ready for work. She got the water running full blast into the tub before padding to the kitchen to make herself a steaming cup of instant coffee. Placing the cup on the edge of the tub, she eased into the tub and laid her head back on her bath pillow. "Now this is living," she said to herself. "The only thing better would be if CC was here to enjoy it with me."

Amid thoughts of CC, she couldn't help but process the facts of the investigation and analyze them. Gwen wondered what Wright was scheming right now and if Kathy's friend, Linda, was justified in being apprehensive about her own safety. She hoped the Planton brothers would put their energies now into laying their sister to rest, instead of continuing the pursuit of her attacker. And where were the other two women? Was there a chance one or both of them were still alive?

Gwen's coffee had gotten cold and her skin shriveled like a prune when she pulled the plug on the drain and toweled herself off. She decided on black jeans, a beige sweater and brown suede blazer. Her short curly hair was a tangled mess, and she did the best she could to get it to lie flat with a dab of hair gel.

Gwen arrived at The Dive at eight fifteen. CC was sitting at the bar tonight, as none of the regulars were playing pool. Reyna wasn't here either and her usual place near the pool tables looked unusually bare without her massive presence.

Gwen nodded and sat three stools to the right of CC. Ben was on the phone, but nodded in acknowledgment and opened a bottle of light beer and set it in front of her while continuing his conversation. He wasn't saying much, but he had a concerned look on his face and grunted from time to time, listening carefully to whatever the caller was telling him.

When he got off the phone five minutes later he said solemnly, "That was TJ. He was supposed to bring Reyna here tonight. Found her at home…she's dead."

"My God!" CC exclaimed. "A heart attack?" she asked, considering the woman's bulk.

"Dunno yet. He called nine-one-one and they'd just arrived. Said she was lying near the doorway, her cart tipped on its side. She had a deep cut somewhere on her head spilling a lot of blood, but she may have hit her head against the wall or door frame."

"I'm so sorry," Gwen said, consoling Ben. "She'd been coming in frequently for quite some time, hadn't she?"

"Gotta be six, seven years at least," Ben said sadly. "She started coming in soon as her youngest moved out of the house. She was kinda our resident shrink...knew all the happenings of everyone, and let us all know if we needed to lend our support. Kinda like a second family here, you know?"

"I understand," Gwen said solemnly.

"She always let me know if someone was getting out of line, too. I've eighty-sixed plenty of rowdy folk on her recommendation."

"I'll miss her, and I've known her only a few days," CC said sadly. "We could take up a collection for her family...you know, help out with the funeral expenses."

"Yeah, that's a good idea," Ben replied. "I know her kids are struggling with their babies and all. Didn't seem like Reyna had much herself."

The bar started filling up and people began reminiscing about Reyna. Even though everybody regarded her as a busybody probing into their personal business, there was a fondness in their voices that revealed she was well-regarded for her big heart and generous spirit. Ben described it best when he said, "She made you laugh regardless of how shitty your day was going."

TJ stumbled into the bar a short time later, looking as though he'd lost his best friend. "Never found no dead person before, and I never wanna go through that again."

"I'm so sorry," CC told him when he pulled a barstool up next to her.

"Them cops that came after I called nine-one-one? They treated me like I done it. Gave me the third degree, they did."

Ben put a bottle of beer in front of TJ and said, "It's on the house, buddy."

"I'll take a shot of that Jack Daniels too, s'long as you're buying."

"That's pretty much routine, isn't it?" CC asked innocently. "You wouldn't want them to let someone get away if they had actually committed a crime. Anyway, on TV the cops always talk to the people hanging around the victim."

"I suppose so," TJ agreed. "Just wishing they didn't have to be so mean about it. I thought for sure I was gonna be arrested. Try explainin' that to the missus...geez, I don't even tell the wife

I play taxi driver for some of the womenfolk." He downed his shot of whiskey in one gulp and took a long swig of his beer.

"Any idea how she died?" Ben asked.

"I don't know, man. There was that blood all over the carpet from a gash just above her eyebrows. Cops whisked me out of there quick like when they came in. Had to talk to them in the garage."

"I mean, did it look like someone attacked her, or she just fell over like her heart stopped or something?" Ben probed.

"I just can't say, Ben. I got kinda shook up seeing her lying there in the first place. Couldn't even find my phone in my pocket, my hands were shaking so bad. Had to use her house phone to call nine-one-one."

"No wonder the cops thought you'd killed her. You left fingerprints all over the damn place!" one of the other men at the bar chimed in.

TJ turned beet-red and said shakily, "You think?"

"No doubt about it," the man kept razzing him. "They'll probably call you back and give you the third degree. Oh man, that's not going to be pleasant."

TJ turned white as a sheet.

"Don't listen to him," Gwen said, getting off her barstool and reading a text message on her cell phone. "He's just kidding you. I'm sure they wouldn't have let you leave if they thought you were guilty of anything."

"She's right, TJ," CC said soothingly. "Don't worry."

"Thanks. Sure hope you girls are right. Hey, Ben. You'd better pour me another shot."

Gwen went into the ladies' room, locking the door behind her. She dialed Brad's number and asked, "What's up?"

"Another one of The Dive's patrons was found dead not long ago."

"Yeah, we heard all about it—in fact, everyone's talking about it at the bar. One of the men from here was supposed to pick her up. He's the one who found her dead and he's telling his story now."

"Did he tell you she was stabbed?" Brad asked.

"No!" Gwen said with alarm. "He said she had a cut on her forehead. He figured she got it from hitting her head when she fell."

"The first responders didn't see it either until they were finally able to turn her over. She was heavyset, so it took some doing to get her on her stomach. Four stab wounds to her abdomen, then some shallow cuts to connect the dots to form a cross."

"Similar to Carole," Gwen replied miserably.

"Just about," Brad agreed.

"Can we keep the crosses out of the press?" Gwen asked. "I don't want to panic the public into thinking we've got a serial killer just yet."

"Too late. One of the woman's sons showed up before they moved the body. He was talking to that loudmouth from the *Scarletsville News* when I left. You know how quickly the press corps jumps when something like this hits the police scanners... like a cobra on its prey."

"Did Doc Maynard say when he'd be doing the autopsy?" Gwen asked.

"Yep. Said I should tell you same time, same place," Brad told her.

"All right. I won't be staying too late if I've got to be at the morgue at six a.m. Hey, I won't be able to clue CC in while I'm here. Give her a call later to bring her up to date, will you?"

"Sure. Catch you tomorrow at the office."

CHAPTER TWENTY-SEVEN

"Too many furrows of fatty tissue would have made it difficult to slice her throat," Doc Maynard was saying to Gwen. "The taut skin across her back would have been the second easiest route for his attack; the first being the stomach area—although there are a lot of folds, the skin is soft and pliable. From the back he would have had the added element of surprise though, I suppose. He's either fairly strong or had help turning her onto her back after she was dead. She weighed in at three hundred and twenty-one and one quarter. Not an easy task to move that kind of dead weight."

Gwen had been running late, having had trouble getting a playful Max to pay attention and do his business on their morning walk. And it was just her luck that Doc was anxious to get started, having had three additional corpses come in during the night. He had begun Reyna's autopsy early, just before Gwen had arrived.

"What about the stomach contents?" Gwen asked.

"Just had eaten…not an hour before her death. Meatloaf and mashed potatoes had barely started digesting. She was taking medications…I found small pieces of some tablets and sent them to the lab for analysis. Considering her size and the color of the tablets, I'm guessing blood pressure and hypoglycemia."

"Knife wounds?"

"Three inches wide, two deep. Looks like the same instrument, but it's hard to tell. If he had used a serrated knife, it would be easier to match."

"So all we really have is the sign of the cross?" Gwen asked, hoping there was more.

"We can hope they find trace evidence on her clothes," Doc offered.

"Nothing came back on Carole's?" Gwen inquired.

"No, not yet anyway," Doc answered.

"Okay. Thanks, Doc," Gwen said grimly.

***

"I think we've found the bar Kathy and Meg frequented," Scott said proudly when the task force met at four p.m. "Actually, the captain led us right to it. It's only three blocks from Meg's apartment."

"He's frequenting bars in that neighborhood?" Brad asked incredulously.

"Yep. In fact, our new recruit was the one who followed him there. After Wright left, Sammy took the photos in and confirmed with the bartender that the women looked familiar. The place is called Tina's Pub."

"Shit." Brad let out a sigh. "I saw several references to Tina's on Facebook, but kept thinking it was a friend of Meg's. Never connected that it was a place and not a person. In fact, I looked for 'Tina' in the address book and didn't find her. Now I know why."

"What time was Wright there?" Gwen asked.

"Entered at three-oh-four and left at five-thirty-three," Scott read from his notes.

"Sammy know what he did for two and a half hours?"

"Yeah. From where he was parked, Sammy could see through one of the not so grimy spots on the window…Drank four Budweisers and was watching a baseball game on the TV over the bar."

"Interesting. And he's sure Wright didn't meet with anyone?" Gwen asked, puzzled.

"Yes," Scott answered with certainty.

"How did the notify go?" Gwen asked CC.

"It was so sad," CC said softly. "They didn't always show it, but those boys really did love their sister. Her mom was inconsolable, but it looked like the brothers will keep close tabs on her for a while. I promised them we'd find Carole's killer. I don't think they'll get in our way."

"It's not an easy thing to do. Thanks for handling it," Gwen said kindly.

"Doesn't get any easier either, no matter how many times you have to break it to the family," Brad added.

"On a positive note." CC brightened. "I found another contact in Meg's address book. I'm just about finished going through it. Most are business contacts and former classmates and co-workers long forgotten. The kind that say, 'Meg who?' and have to think a long while to remember they knew somebody by that name. But one of my last calls was returned by a man named Kyle. Brad, if you remember, you'd know him as Kinky on Facebook and dating and social networking sites."

"Sure, I remember seeing his name."

"Well, turns out he and Meg were an item for about six months. They broke it off, but stayed friends. The best part is that he was actually there, in Meg's apartment, one night when she was freaking out about the man parked in the car across the street," CC said excitedly. "He agreed to meet me at Starbucks at seven tonight."

"Sounds promising," Brad said, sharing her excitement.

"Yeah, we could really use a break in this case," Gwen agreed.

"Did he actually see the man in the car?" Scott asked.

"I don't know yet. When he called, he was running late for work. He said he'd tell me everything tonight. By the way, he's a masseuse and hairstylist by profession. I'm pretty sure he's gay, but just in case I don't make it to The Dive in time, I might be getting a massage. Hmm, maybe a facial too."

Everyone looked at her in shock and surprise.

"Geez, guys. Just kidding," CC laughed.

CHAPTER TWENTY-EIGHT

When Gwen arrived at The Dive at eight thirty, CC had not arrived yet. She was dying to find out what she had found out from the hairstylist, but would have to wait until after they left The Dive.

Gwen ordered a beer and wondered if she should be worrying about CC meeting this guy. After all, who knew what kind of unsavory characters Meg had latched onto. Gwen had been surprised many times by the men whom seemingly straightforward and intelligent women fell in love with. No, she reasoned to herself, CC could take care of herself as well as any other woman Gwen had met on the force. And meeting at Starbucks was hardly dangerous. It wasn't like he had asked to meet her in a dark alley.

"Spaceship back to earth," Ben said and laughed, breaking her reverie. "Girl, you're way out there tonight."

"Sorry. Just daydreaming, I guess," Gwen said, embarrassed.

"It's night now, honey. No daydreaming allowed. The dart team will be here in a half hour or so. I want to see some good play tonight."

"I think we could all use that."

"You know, I was afraid folk would quit coming in with all the freaky stuff going on, but it's just been the opposite. Seems like the family is sticking closer together. I've been busier than hell the past week. Sure, some of 'ems just nosy and coming around to see what's the latest, but mostly, people are real concerned."

"Ben, you realize that's a compliment to you, don't you? You make everyone feel safe, comfortable and taken care of," Gwen told him.

"Well, thank you, Miss Gwen. I think that's the nicest thing anyone's ever said to me. Now go have yourself some fun," he said, nodding to the group coming in the door.

"Yes!"

It was after ten and they were on their second game of darts when CC walked in and sat at the bar. Her face was flushed, almost glowing, and Gwen could tell her meeting had gone well. CC was nearly bursting at the seams to talk, but Gwen could only nod, acknowledging her presence.

Gwen finished the third game and lost miserably. He mind was not on the game. She took the ribbing from her teammates with good humor, laughing with them about her off center shots, and went to the bar to finish her beer.

It was almost midnight and Gwen stifled a few yawns and said her goodbyes. While Ben walked her to her car, she caught CC leaving with TJ at her side. "See you tomorrow," she said, and waved to Ben as he turned to walk inside.

"You be damn careful out there," he grumbled in return.

Gwen's phone rang before she had a chance to fire up her engine. "Your place or mine?" CC giggled. "I'm dying to talk to you."

"Mine?"

"Okay. Race you there?" CC teased.

"No," Gwen laughed. "Take it easy and get there in one piece. I missed you too much to have to wait for an accident report to be written for an unnecessary fender-bender."

As soon as they were inside the door, Gwen grabbed CC by the waist and pulled her close. "Umm, you smell good," she said and kissed her fervently.

"I missed you too, but…" CC said, pushing away. "I'm going to burst if I don't tell you about my meeting with Kyle…I mean Kinky. God, do you believe that's what he wants to be called? Can we sit and have a cup of coffee for a few minutes?"

"Sure," Gwen agreed. "Come into the kitchen and tell me everything."

"Well," CC said, plopping onto one of the kitchen chairs, slipping out of her shoes, and folding her legs under her buttocks. "He's bisexual, or at least was when he dated Meg. He has a boyfriend now, so I guess you'd say he's living the gay lifestyle, although he's monogamous and his boyfriend isn't. He was Meg's friend up until the time she disappeared. You know how everyone said Meg was a good friend and listener? He credits Meg for bringing his feelings for other men out in the open, and even introduced him to the partner he's sharing his life with now. He's not sure it will work out, but at least he's been able to explore his feelings and be honest about who he is."

She leaned forward and propped her head in her hands. "About two weeks before Meg disappeared, she invited him for dinner. When she got up to clear the dishes, she looked out the window above the sink and let out a shriek that he said would have woke the dead. Kinky thought she'd cut herself on a knife or something. She was staring at a black Mercury Cougar…he's sure that's what it was. The man was staring back and…oh, God, Gwen…I think we have sort of a description."

"Sort of a description?" Gwen repeated, as she placed one of the steaming cups in front of CC.

"Well, it was dark, but Kinky said it was an older man with very short hair, almost military style. Of course, sitting down, he couldn't judge the man's height, but was sure he weighed about two hundred or so." CC sighed and her voice dropped to a whisper as she distractedly combed through her hair with her fingers. "I sure hope he can remember something more about the man."

"Well, at least it's something to go on. Would he be able to work with a sketch artist?"

"He doesn't think he saw the facial features that clearly. Another car came down the street and the man sped off. What he was one hundred percent sure of was that the man was there only to stare at Meg through the window."

"What about hypnotism?" Gwen suggested. "Maybe he'd remember more that way?"

"Could be. I'll call him tomorrow and suggest it."

"Anything else?" Gwen asked.

"Yep." CC slid off her chair and snuggled onto Gwen's lap. She kissed her lips gently and leisurely, making Gwen dizzy with desire.

"Good thing I'm sitting down, woman," Gwen said softly. "You make my knees go weak."

"And I've only just begun."

***

Gwen awoke with her nose nestled in CC's long blond hair and one arm draped across her shoulders. She lay very still so as not to wake CC, remembering the fireworks of their lovemaking. Every time with CC was better than the last. They were now completely comfortable in each other's arms and were learning the other's likes, fine-tuning their dance and bringing each other to heights Gwen had only dreamed of.

Gwen knew without asking that CC was still tentative about making a commitment. Understandably, after being in a relationship where she had felt boxed in and trapped, she enjoyed the freedom of having her own place, and coming and going as she pleased. Gwen would jump at the chance to claim CC as her partner, and be proud to marry her if that were a legal option, but she already loved her too much to force her into making a decision. Not being a patient person by nature, Gwen forced her feelings to the side and just let things be. She enjoyed being with CC whenever possible, and loved watching her bloom and knew she would grow with their relationship in her own time.

CC snuggled closer in her slumber and Gwen pulled her tightly against her body. She stifled a yawn and soon was sound asleep again.

CHAPTER TWENTY-NINE

"I'm anxious to get to the office and make some calls," CC said over breakfast. After they'd gotten up and showered, Gwen had made French toast and bacon, two of the few things she actually liked to cook.

"Sure. We can go in early. I should have the autopsy reports on my desk to review," Gwen answered. "Hopefully the lab has finished analyzing their clothing too."

"I've got a nagging fear about Linda. I'm sure she's okay, but I just want to follow up to let her know I'm still here if she needs me. Then I'll give Kinky a call and see if he's willing to be hypnotized to try to come up with a composite of the man watching Meg."

"Good idea," Gwen said, clearing the table.

"Let me help you," CC said, getting up. "I slept like a baby last night. I'm energized and feel wonderful today," she said, stretching her arms over her head.

"If you have that much energy, maybe you'd like to go with me to take Max for a walk," Gwen suggested.

"I'd love to. He's such a gentle dog...just what I'd pick out if I was looking for one. I'm not though, so don't get any ideas," CC said, and laughed after seeing Gwen's hopeful face.

"I guess Max is around enough that I don't need my own, but I've thought about getting a smaller breed. I'd love to have a lap dog...one I can pick up and carry with me. You know, the side of the bed you sleep on gets awfully cold and lonely when you're not here. I could snuggle up to the dog and pretend it was you. The problem is, we work so many long hours and are gone so much of the time."

"Hmm...I'm sure Max would enjoy the company of another dog when you're not here. I'd share it with you, like you share Max with Pierre," CC said, getting excited about the prospect. "Let's just go see what's available at the shelter this weekend. We don't have to actually bring one home; just do some window-shopping."

"My problem with window-shopping," Gwen remarked, "is that I'd end up bringing three or four home with me. I feel so sorry for those caged pups. Dogs need room to roam, toys to chew on, socks to tear apart. I'm warning you, I'm a sucker for those sad, lonely faces. But sure, we can go Saturday if you'd like."

"Oh, let's do it!" CC said decisively.

***

When they got to the office, CC took off to make her telephone calls while Gwen plowed through a mound of mail and several envelopes from the lab.

Her spirits lifted when she read that the green carpet fibers found on the clothes of Carole were identifiable; they'd been sent for further forensic testing. It wasn't much, but at least they had something traceable to work with.

Making a side-by-side comparison of the photographs he'd taken at the autopsies, Doc Maynard had written that he was ninety-eight percent certain that the same weapon inflicted the knife wounds on both victims. He wrote at length about the superficial cuts depicting the cross on the torsos being microscopically identical.

Gwen imagined Doc getting up during the middle of the night to test or measure something on his cadavers. He'd once told her his best ideas came during sleep, and the security guards attested to the fact that Doc crept into the morgue at all times of the day and night. New guards were often startled to see the old man walking the hallways with his tape recorder in hand at odd hours.

There were a few messages Gwen needed to return, and it was nearly one p.m. by the time CC came back to the office.

"Kinky agreed to do it," CC told her. "It's all set up for tomorrow. I haven't been able to reach Linda though. I'm kind of worried, so I thought I'd take a drive over to her place."

"Sure. You have plenty of time. Our task force meeting isn't until four. You want to grab some lunch before you go?" Gwen asked.

"No. Let me just get this behind me so I can alleviate this annoying uneasiness," CC replied.

"Okay. Can you give me a call when you find her?"

"Will do," CC answered, hurrying out.

Gwen got back to her paperwork and forgot that she was going to run down to the cafeteria for a sandwich. The autopsy and lab reports didn't contain any other helpful information, but Gwen read each one over again to make sure they were committed to her memory and that she hadn't missed anything important.

About an hour later Gwen's phone rang. CC sounded relieved. "Linda's having problems with her phone and can't get it to recharge. She's fine and we're going out to have lunch. You're welcome to join us, if you'd like."

"Nah. I really need to get through the rest of this paperwork. I'll just grab something from downstairs, but thanks for asking. I'm glad Linda's okay and nothing's wrong. Enjoy your lunch."

"Thanks. I'm so relieved. I just want to find this creep before someone else gets hurt," CC whispered, walking out of Linda's earshot.

"I'm with you. See you later," Gwen said.

Scott knocked on her office door. "Got a minute?" He was beaming.

"Yeah, sure. What's up?"

"I know we don't have a chance very often to talk about personal stuff, but I just wanted to tell you that we just found out Katie is pregnant."

"Wow, that's great! Congratulations!" Gwen knew they'd been trying to conceive for at least a couple years. Scott had been dragged from one fertility clinic to another by his wife. Although he didn't seem to mind. He was as anxious to have a child as she was.

"Guess we can cancel the adoption process." Scott was still grinning broadly.

"When's she due?" Gwen asked.

"In early January. It's perfect...our New Year's baby. We're going to call her Gracie if it's a girl."

"Cool. I like that. Come on, I'll buy you lunch to celebrate," Gwen offered.

"Uh, I just ate with Katie, but tell you what...you can buy me a Coke."

"Deal."

***

By four everyone was assembled in Gwen's office. She gave them the details of the autopsy and laboratory results she'd reviewed that morning.

When it was CC's turn, she brought the men up to date on her interview with Kinky and the plan to have him hypnotized. "Linda is still freaking out, but I think she'll be okay. I think her imagination is working overtime. She has the feeling someone is following her, but has never seen anyone anywhere close to her when she gets her goose bumps."

"We've alerted the patrol unit in her area. They'll swing by a couple extra times each shift," Brad advised them.

Gwen's phone rang and she listened briefly and then advised the caller she was on her way.

"We've got another body. They think it's Meg. A couple of high school kids found her in a drainage ditch on the outskirts of town. She's been there a couple days and it won't be pretty."

"I want to get any evidence we can find to the lab ASAP," CC said, on her way to the door.

"I can drive," Scott said, grabbing his jacket.

"I'll get in touch with Doc Maynard and the chief. Call me as soon as you have more information. I'll try to hold the press at bay," Brad offered.

"Will do," Gwen said, following CC and Scott out the door.

CHAPTER THIRTY

It turned out Doc Maynard was in the neighborhood, and after receiving Brad's call, beat them to the crime scene. He was crouched over the body as Gwen approached. Meg looked like a small, sleeping child, curled up with her knees nearly touching her chin.

"I don't think this is the murder site," Doc remarked as he looked up at Gwen. "Not enough blood, and with her throat slashed, there'd have been plenty."

"Any other wounds?" she asked.

"Yep. Carbon copy of Carole Planton with the stab to the abdomen and superficial cuts forming the cross."

"How long has she been out here?" CC asked, crouching next to him.

"Less than a week. No more than four, possibly five, days is my guess," he answered.

Maynard quickly got back to his work. "Look here, Gwen," he said. "Looks like the same green fibers on her shirt we've found at the other crime scenes." He carefully plucked them from the body and bagged them.

Gwen said, "And there's soil stuck to her jeans which doesn't look like the surrounding landscape. It looks like potting soil."

"When will you have time to do the autopsy, Doc?" Scott asked.

"I believe I'll go back to my office now. I'll complete the autopsy tonight when the crime scene unit finishes and my people deliver the corpse. Tomorrow's Saturday, and I have a birthday party for my granddaughter to attend," he said.

"Gwen, I'll attend this one, if you don't mind," Scott said. "I know you and CC need to get to The Dive. Maybe I can even get Doc's expertise to fill me in on what I can expect with Katie's pregnancy. I'll call Brad and have him cover the parking lot at The Dive."

"Sure. That works out great," Gwen replied. "I appreciate you going."

"I'll drop you women off at the precinct, and Doc, I'll meet you at the morgue."

"Fine, sonny. I can give you a few pointers…so you say your wife's pregnant, huh? My, my! I remember when my Bessie had her first one…"

CC giggled and Gwen whispered in her ear, "Scott has no idea what a long night he has ahead of him."

***

The Dive was packed when Gwen arrived. CC was already playing pool. It had taken Gwen longer than she had expected, since the parking lot at the precinct had been packed with reporters. She had had to weed her way through the throng yelling, "No comment" all the way to her car. So much for Brad keeping the press at bay. She knew it wasn't his fault, but she hated the mob scene with journalists more than any other aspect of her police work.

Gwen hadn't seen any reporters at the site where Meg had been found, but there had been a few onlookers pressed against the crime scene tape. Someone must have tipped off the newspapers and television stations. The story was already being passed around at the bar, and Gwen ordered a beer and listened. Most of the patrons had known Meg fairly well, at least in comparison to the other missing girls. With the exception of Reyna, the others were only acquaintances. There was a subdued atmosphere as they mourned the loss of their friend. They were befuddled by the knowledge that this was happening, and horrified that the women were being found dead. Someone had finally burst their balloon of hope, and replaced it with deep sadness.

The TV over the bar flashed to the now empty drainage ditch where Meg had been found. Yellow crime scene tape floated eerily in the darkness. A reporter had somehow connected the murders of Carole, Reyna and now Meg, to The Dive.

Ben looked on in horror, no doubt thinking that his business would be ruined. "Damn it all," he said to Gwen. "I loved those women like my own sisters. We looked after them when they needed looking after. Ain't the fault of The Dive what happened to 'em."

"I know, Ben. I'm sure when the police catch the murderer, no one will blame you just because they were your customers. Just wait til this blows over," Gwen said soothingly.

"Promise?" he said hopefully.

"Promise."

"Okay. You get out there and play your game. They waitin' on you."

"You got it. And Ben? This one's for you!"

She joined the dart players and won three straight games. When she was finished, she felt as if she'd worked off some of the stress. She had renewed resolve and determination. She would not only avenge the murders for the families, she would keep the promise she'd made to Ben.

CHAPTER THIRTY-ONE

Gwen and CC had stayed at The Dive until after midnight. Afterward CC decided to follow Gwen home so they could spend Saturday together. Gwen found that Scott had faxed the autopsy report on Meg to her well after eleven p.m., so it had indeed been a long night for him. When you got Doc talking he could go on for hours.

They perused the report, but there was nothing new to send them in a different direction or help find the killer. They hoped the lab could give them more information to work with.

They were still discussing the case as they got into bed, bouncing back and forth different strategies. CC started snoring softly in her arms. Gwen smiled, reached over and turned off the light, and snuggled in beside her.

***

CC woke first the following morning and slid quietly out of bed without waking Gwen. She padded to the kitchen in her bare feet and a robe she had found hanging behind the bathroom door, and got to work. She whipped up pancake batter and then made a pot of coffee. She found a container of frozen strawberries in the freezer, which she defrosted in the microwave to spoon over the pancakes. When the pancakes were golden brown, she put everything on a tray and walked back to the bedroom. Gwen was yawning and stretching her arms over her head, her short hair sticking out in all directions. She was just barely awake.

"Wake up, hon. We've got lots to do today!" CC said cheerfully.

"Huh?"

"Sit up. I'm serving breakfast in bed," CC ordered.

"No shit? Cool!" Gwen said, blinking the sleep out of her eyes and fluffing up the pillows behind her.

CC put the tray between them and they dug in hungrily.

"You're a good cook. These pancakes are wonderful," Gwen said with her mouth full.

"It's my grandmother's recipe...my favorite breakfast. I was surprised to find the strawberries," CC said, taking a bite.

"I usually put them on ice cream, but this is much better," Gwen said, licking her fingers.

"So, what do you want to do today?" Gwen asked.

"I want to go to the animal shelter. I've been thinking about it since you mentioned it...can we just go look. Please?"

Gwen laughed. "Of course we can just go look, but we'd better stop at the pet store and pick up some supplies for our 'just look.' I have to pick up food and treats for Max anyway."

Gwen put the tray on the nightstand and asked huskily, "Do we have time for this?" and she kissed CC passionately.

"Umm...yes!" CC agreed wholeheartedly.

Afterward, they got up and cleaned the kitchen, fed Max, and took off for the pet supply store. They filled the cart with dog food and treats, shampoo and hair conditioner, and a small dog bed made of lambskin. CC picked out a light blue collar with tiny white dog bones on it and a matching leash. They had a hard time limiting the number of squeaky toys they wanted to buy; there was such a large variety and they were all adorable. Laughing in the aisle, they played with several of the toys before finally deciding on four smaller ones and a large, purple, stuffed rabbit for Max. They loaded everything into her trunk, and they headed to the animal shelter.

"I'm kind of nervous," CC admitted. "What if they don't like me or are afraid to come to me?"

"These poor souls will eat up any attention you give them. You will be saving them from being caged twenty-four/seven and they'll never forget that. Besides, how could they not like you?" Gwen replied, squeezing her hand.

"I feel like I'm adopting a baby!" CC exclaimed.

Gwen laughed. "In a sense, that's exactly what you're doing."

When they got to the shelter, the two women walked hand in hand through several large buildings, each with a variety of breeds and sizes. They agreed some were too large, several too hyper, and a few very unfriendly. Some barked at them furiously and others were meek and shied away.

"I didn't know this would be so hard," CC complained.

"You'll know when you find the right one for you," Gwen said encouragingly.

They walked through three more buildings, and at the end of the last one was a cage with two small, white terriers. They knelt down and put their hands against the cage while the two pups came excitedly to them, licking their fingers and wagging their tails.

"Oh, Gwen. These guys are adorable," CC cried out.

"Says they're brothers. Both are already neutered, so they're ready to take home," Gwen said, reading the paper enclosed in a plastic sheath. "They're about a year old."

"Can we take them both?" CC begged.

"I don't see why not." She grinned. "We'll have to stop at the pet store and get another collar, leash and bed."

They found an attendant, a young dark-haired volunteer, who took the dogs out of the cage and handed each woman a leash. In a small caged area, the boys romped and played fetch with a ball, but kept coming back to the women, anxious to get more attention. They rubbed their noses against their legs when they stopped petting them.

"I think they like me," CC said, grinning from ear to ear.

"Then it's a done deal. Let's get the paperwork finished," Gwen said, waving for the attendant.

"We'll take both of them," Gwen said definitely.

"I'm so glad," the young woman said eagerly. "We were afraid we'd have to split them up. They're both such nice dogs…very well behaved and potty trained too. The owner had to move to an assisted living complex after breaking a hip and couldn't take the dogs with her."

"Thanks for the information," Gwen replied. "Have they had all their shots?"

"Yes, we give them all booster shots when they come in, make sure they're microchipped and neutered. You'll also get a free veterinary visit. You'll get their papers too—they're both pedigree terriers. The owner had sired them from her previous terrier."

"Uh, does that make them more expensive?" CC asked hesitantly.

"No, we charge just one standard fee for each adoption. It's just nice to be able to find all these guys new homes." The attendant smiled.

It took about forty-five minutes to fill out the necessary paperwork. Afterward CC stayed in the car and played with the pups while Gwen ran into the pet store to get the additional supplies they'd need.

When they got home, they let the dogs roam around the house, sniffing and making sure they were comfortable in their new environment.

"We've got to name them," CC said, squeaking a small teddy bear to get the pups' attention.

"Any ideas?" Gwen asked.

"Well, the smaller of the two looks like a peanut...we could call him Peanut."

Gwen laughed. "How about Cashew then for the other? So we'll have Peanut and Cashew."

"Perfect," CC laughed.

"I'd like to cordon off an area out back for them to play in. It'll be warm enough soon for them to spend time outside. I'll get some fencing material and stakes and put them around the big oak tree so they have shade," Gwen said.

"That would be great. I'll take them to the park while you're getting the supplies," CC offered.

"You don't mind dog-sitting my half of the family?" Gwen teased.

"I just love them to pieces already, Gwen. I'm not going to want to leave them for one second," she said, picking Peanut up and letting him lick her face.

Max walked in cautiously and the two little pups started barking.

"Oh boy," Gwen said. "Max, this is Peanut and this is Cashew. They're your new playmates."

Max inched forward and sniffed the two little guys, who danced around the bigger dog, doing plenty of sniffing of their own. Max's tail started wagging as they all settled down.

"Looks like they're already friends!" CC said happily.

"I think the little guys will be good for Max. He'll get more exercise following them around. And look, they want to play with him." Gwen laughed when Cashew dropped one of the toys at Max's feet.

"Oh, we forgot to give Max his new toy!" CC exclaimed, getting the purple rabbit out of one of the bags.

Max grabbed the rabbit and started chomping down to make it squeak, while the two little guys jumped around him, enjoying the action but staying a safe distance away.

"Well, if I'm going to get the pen done today, I'd better get moving. Have fun!"

"You know I will," CC replied, already lying on the floor on her tummy to scratch the boys behind their ears and roughhouse with them.

***

By dinnertime Gwen had finished the outside play area, a twelve by twelve square foot fenced area with the tree in the center. CC had run home to pack a bag with enough clothes for a few days. They decided they'd keep the dogs at Gwen's house for a week, and take them to CC's to get them used to her place the following week. It was agreed that they'd always keep the two together, and when the dogs were used to both places, they would take turns keeping them.

They ordered pizza for dinner and when everyone was exhausted, they put one of the doggie beds on each side of their bed. Gwen and CC kissed and hugged, too tired to make love and Gwen turned off the light. Within two seconds they felt a plop at the foot of the bed as one, then the other dog joined them, snuggling against their feet. They started laughing and finally fell asleep, all four nestled closely together.

CHAPTER THIRTY-TWO

Sunday the women enjoyed playing with the new pups and invited Gwen's neighbor, Pierre, and his dog Max over for dinner. CC made a pork roast with mashed potatoes, green beans, sweet corn on the cob, and a cherry cobbler for dessert. Gwen gave each of the dogs a rawhide bone to keep them occupied while they ate. They were happy to hear that Pierre was off work the next three days, so he could keep an eye on all three dogs while they were at work. After dinner they all took off for the park, and laughed as the smaller dogs tried to beat Max to the Frisbee Pierre was throwing across the grass for Max to catch. With shorter legs, Cashew was a close second, and Peanut kept stopping dead in his tracks, distracted by every sound around him.

That afternoon the women moved the dog beds to the living room, where the boys liked to take short naps during the day. They knew after the first night that there was no way to stop the boys from sleeping on the bed, and besides, they enjoyed waking with cold noses and furry bodies rubbing against their skin. Both pups were constantly doing silly things to keep them laughing. They played hard and demanded their constant attention, which they were happy to give. Then, like little toy trains having lost their steam, the adorable little boys would lie down and close their eyes.

***

Monday morning came far too quickly, and CC and Gwen were sad to leave the boys behind. They closed off the door to the bedroom, and scattered toys around the living room for them to play with. It nearly broke CC's heart to see Peanut's big, brown, sad eyes staring at her longingly when they finally closed the door at eleven a.m. to leave for work.

On the way to the precinct, CC suggested, "Hey, I'd like to stop at that bar Sammy saw Wright going into. He can't stop us from innocently being someplace that he frequents. I mean, if we ran into each other in a restaurant or something, hey, it's a free country."

"Great idea. I think Scott said it was Tina's Pub, but we can double-check at the task force meeting. Why don't we go before heading to The Dive? If Wright does show up, Sammy should be close behind to back us up."

"And if he doesn't show up, it would be the perfect opportunity to ask around about Meg and Kathy," CC offered.

Scott was already in Gwen's office when they arrived, so they firmed up their plans to check out the bar. When that was settled, they started ribbing Scott about his hours with Doc Maynard.

"Jeepers," Scott said, shaking his head. "The man has three daughters and a ton of grandchildren. I had to hear about every one of the pregnancies, all the births, and I got a rundown of how wonderful they all are now. I feel like I'm already part of the family, and I've not met one of them."

"Doc is a wonderful man, but he is a talker when you get him going," Gwen said.

Brad walked in and the four got busy and started talking about the investigation. "The green fibers the evidence techs found are a definite match. All are from the same carpet manufacturer, and used in Chevrolet trunks," Brad confirmed.

"Interesting," Gwen commented. "We know the women were transported after death, so it has to be a big enough car to fit a body in the trunk. That leaves out hatchbacks and other compact models."

"If he's a big man, he wouldn't be driving a small car anyway," Scott piped in. "I have trouble driving my wife's Fiat. There just isn't enough leg room."

"We've got some samples going to the manufacturers to see if we can narrow it down more," Brad told them.

Gwen filled Brad in on their plans to visit Tina's Pub. "Sounds like a good plan," he said. "Just be careful."

***

Gwen and CC got to Tina's just past eight. They found a table in the back of the dimly lit dining room and ordered Cokes and burgers. They ate slowly, talking about the dogs. They giggled softly about how cute they had looked when they'd stopped home that afternoon to feed and walk them.

"What a difference between this bar and The Dive," CC remarked. "It's practically deserted. They don't have pool tables or dart boards to attract the late crowd."

"The food is good though," Gwen said, taking another bite of her cheeseburger.

"Yeah, I'll agree with you there. But it's dark...and, I don't know...kind of dreary. It's not a place I'd like to spend a lot of time in."

"Yeah, it's not my kind of place either. Doesn't look like Wright is going to show up anyway, and there's no one at the bar to talk to about the missing women. Let's get the check and get going."

There was only one other occupied table, at the other end of the dining room. The waitress was standing there and gabbing with a young couple, oblivious to her other customers. "This might take awhile," CC fumed.

"Shhh. Wright just walked in. He's sitting with his back to us at the bar," Gwen whispered.

"Oh, shit. Are you going to go over and talk to him?"

"No. Let's just sit here quietly and watch. He didn't notice us, so let's pretend we didn't see him come in. Just keep talking quietly."

Wright ordered a drink, drank it quickly, and ordered another. From what Gwen could see, it looked like brandy and Coke. He either wanted a quick buzz or was nervous, because he was already half finished with his second drink.

Ten minutes later, as he slowed down and was sipping his third cocktail, another man walked in. He didn't sit, but stood next to Wright and ordered a stein of beer from the bartender.

"Hey, isn't that the creepy DA from the fourth floor?" CC asked.

"Yeah, it's District Attorney Algier. I heard he's tight with Judge Garmer."

Gwen took out her cell phone and discreetly shot off a couple pictures of the two men.

While the bartender's back was turned, Wright handed Algier an envelope which he folded in half and quickly pocketed. The bartender returned and put the beer on the counter, which Algier grabbed, drank half in one gulp, and after throwing a couple dollars on the bar, quickly left.

"Drugs?" CC whispered.

"No, from my angle I saw green when he folded the envelope. It's got to be a bribe, and there's no doubt in my mind Garmer will see some of that money. No wonder Wright got such a sweet deal from the judge."

"Uh-oh," CC said, sinking lower in her seat. "I think he spotted us."

"Just remember what you told me. We have as much right to be here as he does," Gwen said firmly, trying to keep her voice from quivering.

Wright stormed over to their table, his fists clenched at his sides and his eyes bulging with fury.

"You following me again, Detective Meyers?" he raged. "You're a disgrace to the police force, and I'm going to report this."

"What are you going to report, sir? That we came into a bar for burgers and Cokes?" Gwen said smugly, keeping her cool.

"No, that you're harassing me," he spat.

"I have witnesses to the fact that I never said a word until you came to my table and started yelling at me," she said, indicating the young couple and waitress, who were staring at them with shocked expressions. The waitress looked like she couldn't make up her mind whether to run, call the cops, or leave well enough alone.

"I'll get you for this, Meyers, if it's the last thing I do," he snarled, then turned and stormed out of the bar, slamming the door behind him.

"I'd like to pay my check now," Gwen said, taking advantage of finally having the attention of the waitress.

"Huh? Oh sure," she replied, still obviously shaken. "Did you know that guy?"

"I've run into him a few times. What about you? He come in here often?" Gwen asked.

"Yeah, I think so. He's not one of the regulars, but he comes in from time to time. Always at odd times though, and never when it's busy."

"Do you recognize any of these women?" Gwen asked, pulling out the photo spread from her pocket.

"Uh, yeah." She pointed to the picture of Kathy. "That one was with the man who just left. I remember because they were at one of my tables arguing."

"Any of the others?" Gwen probed.

"Maybe that one," she said, pointing to Meg's picture. "I'm not real sure, but she may have been here a few times. Neither one came in that often. Hey, you guys cops?"

"Yes. Both of these women were murdered, so if you think of anything else, could you give me a call?" Gwen said, handing her a card.

"Oh no!" the woman gasped. "I had no idea. So you think the man that left had something to do with it?"

"We're in the early stages of our investigation," Gwen said. "I recommend that if he comes in again, you don't let on you know anything. Just act normally, and if anything seems strange, don't hesitate to call me."

"Oh yes, I'll certainly do that," the woman said nervously, shoving the card into her apron pocket.

As Gwen and CC were leaving, they noticed the waitress back at the young couple's table. She was whispering and her hands were flying in frantic gestures. The couple was listening with rapt attention, completely absorbed.

"Well, I guess we don't have to worry about Wright getting the welcome mat next time he comes in," Gwen chuckled.

"I'll bet that waitress gives you a call each and every time he sets foot in the door from now on," CC said and laughed along with her.

CHAPTER THIRTY-THREE

The following morning Gwen was summoned to Chief Ziegler's office. She hurried to meet with him, anxious to fill him in on her suspicions.

As soon as she arrived, he ushered her into his office and slammed the door. "I've got a complaint against you, Detective. Harassing people now, are we?" he said angrily.

"If you're talking about Wright, I was just eating dinner before heading for my stakeout," Gwen protested.

"That's not what it says here. He says you've been following him and made a scene at the restaurant. He's accusing you of threatening him and trying to coerce others into falsely accusing him of misconduct."

"That's bullshit, Chief. I admit, he's been a person of interest because, well…his name keeps coming up again in my investigation, but he's the one who caused the scene. I have witnesses," Gwen said firmly.

He looked somewhat mollified. "Now what is it that you have on him?" the chief inquired.

Gwen explained about the telephone book and that Kathy and Meg had been meeting at Tina's Pub before they disappeared. She told him everything the waitress had said about seeing Kathy and the captain arguing in the bar, and showed him the pictures she'd taken of Wright and Algier. "Chief, something smells rotten here, and I've got to find out what it is."

He was staring at the photos. "I have to agree there may be more to this than meets the eye, but I want you to back away from Wright. Let me know where and when you expect him, and I'll put someone else on the case to watch him. It's too dangerous for you to get near him. You can still call the shots, but I don't want you within striking distance of him, understood?"

Gwen filled the chief in on the new recruit, Sammy, who had been following Wright since his release.

"I know the young man. Very pleasant and professional. He'll go a long way. I'll have someone team up with Sammy to cover Wright's movements. Does that work for you?"

"I appreciate it," Gwen said.

"Just remember, Gwen. This is getting very dangerous and Captain Wright is gunning for you. Keep your eyes and ears open, but be safe. Now that's an order!" he said, smiling.

"Thanks, Chief. And I appreciate you believing in me. I think we're getting closer. We've got a good team."

"I know you do. Now get back to work," he said, slapping her on the shoulder.

Gwen hurried back to her office, anxious to let the others know about the latest with Wright and his accusations.

"He must have something he's hiding to get so upset by you being at that bar," Brad said thoughtfully.

"And he's getting desperate, because you're always just one step behind him, Gwen," CC added.

"It doesn't make sense that he'd lie," Scott chimed in. "He knows you work for Ziegler. Does he really think anyone will believe him over you?"

"Actually, when I went into the chief's office, he believed Wright's story. Without those photos he'd still believe Wright over me. Let there be no mistake, Wright is a liar and he's good at it. He's been covering his tracks for years with his corruption and alliances with the underground. He believes he can outsmart us all and has the upper hand. Those are the weaknesses we need to capitalize on. We need to move one step ahead of him and watch him hang himself on his cocky attitude."

"What do you suggest?" CC asked.

"Well, the chief doesn't want any of us following Wright. Scott, make sure Sammy tells you about every move Wright makes and report back to the rest of us. I think the rest of us should cozy up with his alliances. And Scott, see if DA Algier wants to have a beer with you. You can boast about how your cases always get priority in the lab and how you work hand in hand with the chemists. I'm sure someone like Algier would love to have someone on the inside to phony some of his results," Gwen said, walking back and forth as she talked. "Brad, isn't your daughter the same age as Judge Garmer's granddaughter? Find out what activities he goes to with his family and enjoy doing the same with yours…paid for by the department. CC, you and I will look up a few old cases. We're looking for anything connecting Wright, Algier and Garmer. And DA Fellerman owes me a few favors. Somehow, we've got to find probable cause to get into the trunk of Wright's car and snip a few fibers."

They all got busy with their assigned tasks, and the rest of the day flew by. It was after six p.m. when Gwen looked up from her stack of files. "CC, what do you think about stopping by the house for a bite to eat? That way we can check in with Pierre and the pups before we head out to The Dive."

"Yeah, I'm famished. We haven't eaten since breakfast," CC said, rubbing her belly. "If I drink one more cup of that rotten coffee on an empty stomach, I'm going to puke."

"Okay, let's get you some food."

Peanut and Cashew were waiting at the door for them, wagging their tails and full of energy. They jumped up on Gwen's and CC's legs and danced around their feet with excitement. Getting down on her knees, CC was smothered with kisses.

"Sure is nice to be missed," Gwen said laughing.

"Gosh, you'd think we'd been gone a week. Just look at those little tails wagging and their kisses are so sweet," CC said, cooing to the boys.

Pierre came to the door and smiled. "So there are your little monsters. I was wondering where they'd run off to."

"Oh-oh," Gwen said. "Did they do something wrong?"

"Found the dog door between our two places in no time flat. Maybe they watched Max going through. Anyway, I had a pile of papers on my den floor I was going to shred...they saved me the trouble. Then they headed to my bathroom and made confetti out of my toilet paper."

"We're so sorry, Pierre. Do you want me to close the dog door during the day?" Gwen asked.

"Nah. After I got everything cleaned up, I went through and puppy-proofed the place. Been a long time since I did that! Actually, it's a lot of fun having them around...they are a couple of characters. And Max is much more active, keeps him from sleeping all day. He's enjoying the little guys too."

"Well, sorry about the mess, Pierre. Let me know if there's anything we can do to make it up to you," CC said.

"Tell you what," Pierre said with a twinkle in his eyes. "Next time you make another one of those superb roasts, you can invite me for dinner again."

CHAPTER THIRTY-FOUR

The following day it seemed as if everything was going at a whirlwind pace. They were all working overtime on their assignments, and Gwen and CC had brought a stack of files home to go over in the morning before they went into the precinct. They decided to make it part of their evening routine to go home and check on the dogs before heading to The Dive, so they wanted to make sure they had plenty of work on hand after eating dinner, feeding the boys, taking them on their walk, and before heading out again. Going through the old case files was slow and tedious work, and so far they hadn't found anything linking the three men together.

At their task force meeting, everyone was hopeful that they were onto something and that the case would be solved soon. There was a nervous tension in the air, as if everyone was expecting the investigation to crack wide open and the perps exposed.

Brad laughed. "Last night my daughter Angela and her two friends needed a ride out to Fairfield High to watch a big soccer match. Turns out there's a big rivalry between Fairfield which my daughter attends, and Oakridge, where I found out Garmer's granddaughter goes to school. I decided to do some surveillance and sat right behind Judge Garmer and his daughter. About halfway through the game, who shows up but that scumbag Algier. I couldn't hear all they were saying, but Gwen, you were right about some of that money finding its way into Garmer's hands. First thing Algier did was hand him the magic envelope."

Scott was bursting at the seams for his turn to share with the group. "I called Sammy and asked him to meet me at the game. He was sitting on the other side of Garmer's daughter. He caught Garmer saying 'the situation hasn't been sufficiently satisfied.' Sammy thinks they're trying to extort more money from Wright. From the look on his face, Algier wasn't happy about it, but told Garmer he'd get back to him.

"Algier didn't stay for the whole game, and I followed him to The Brat Stop when he left," Scott continued. "I sat next to him and ordered a beer. After he was settled and chomping down on his brat, I told him he looked familiar. He straightened up and gave me the 'holier than thou' routine about how important he was in the DA's office. I told him I worked as a liaison between the detectives and the laboratory. His ears perked up and he bought me a beer, but didn't ask for any help. At least not yet."

"That's great work, Scott," Gwen said. "Keep on it."

"I just found a file before the meeting which might be of interest," CC said next. "It's a case that came up before Judge Garmer about a month ago. Algier was the district attorney assigned to the case, and a businessman by the name of Viceroy was claiming extortion by a patrolman named Finley. Sorry guys, this gets murky in the file, but I checked the roster, and Finley worked for Wright. Of course, all charges were dropped quickly.

In fact, it looks like most of the proceedings are missing from the file."

"What happened to the patrol officer...Finley?" Gwen asked.

"I called one of my contacts at the North Precinct," CC replied. "As far as he knows, it's business as usual. Finley is still on the job."

"Brad, can you see if you can find Viceroy? See if he can fill you in on the details," Gwen asked.

"Umm...I did a quick search," CC cut in. "He died of a heart attack two weeks after the hearing."

"Damn," Gwen whistled under her breath. "Okay, then see if he has any family, or maybe a business partner, who knows anything about the case. If he was angry enough to take it all the way to court, he must have let off some steam with someone."

"I'm on it," Brad said enthusiastically.

"One more thing," Scott added. "There was an unfortunate situation with Wright's car last night. Both back tires were slashed. They were flat as pancakes when Wright tried to drive off this morning, so it's being towed to Chuck's Garage. They do a lot of work for the force, so the captain should get a really good deal on two new tires, and Sammy thought he'd give his buddy over there a hand. As long as he's at it, we'll have our fibers from Wright's trunk within a couple hours. I have the lab standing by."

"We need evidence, but be careful we go through the proper channels," Gwen warned. "I don't want anything getting thrown out in court by sloppy detective work, or because we've obtained evidence by illegal means."

Gwen's phone rang. She listened, staring grimly at the team around her. They'd found the body of the third missing woman.

**

Amy Farley's body had been found by a neighbor who had been walking his dog in an empty field not far from the downtown area. The young man was clearly distraught and told them his dog had been pulling at his leash, trying to get him to go in that direction for about a week. He was always in a hurry to get the dog walked so he could get to work, and he had been ignoring the dog's protests. The past two days he smelled something awful coming from that direction, but again, he'd been in a hurry and kept the dog on the path he was accustomed to walking him. He figured it had to be a dead bird or cat, and the last thing he wanted to do was let his black Labrador retriever bring it home. Today he had the day off, so he figured he would let the dog show him where the animal was, and he could come back later and bury it. A dead body was the last thing he'd expected to find.

Amy was a big woman, an Amazon, the patrons at The Dive had called her. She was nearly six feet tall and weighed almost two hundred pounds. Whoever had killed her had to have a fair amount of strength. Just dragging her out of a car would have been a major accomplishment. Like the others, her throat was slashed and her belly split open.

Doc Maynard arrived and confirmed the woman had been dead about a week, give or take a day or two.

Just as in the other murders, CC was able to bag several green fibers from the dead woman's hair and clothing. When she finished her examination, she stood and addressed Doc Maynard. "I guess I have to take my turn. When are you planning on performing the autopsy?"

Gwen couldn't help but laugh at CC's nervous gesture, but stifled her grin as best as she could. CC was trying so hard to be a good sport, do her share, and not appear rattled by the prospect of viewing the body being taken apart piece by piece by Doc Maynard. Her posture and expression made Gwen think of one of the pups shirking away after being disciplined.

"We can do it as soon as the crime scene techs are finished. The sooner the better, don't you think?"

"Uh, I guess so. I haven't attended too many, Doc."

"Oh, don't worry. I'll be gentle with you," he said, taking her hand and leading her away. "Now, over the years I've led hundreds of recruits through the fascinating process of autopsying the body. We can so often gain such a terrific insight as to who the person was and how they conducted their life. There's such a wonderful story told by the skeleton, muscles and internal organs; I never cease being amazed at the outstanding handiwork of our Creator. Usually the bigger they are, the harder it is for them.

You're just a little thing, and I'm guessing you have a fairly strong constitution, so you'll do just fine."

When they were out of earshot, Gwen let out her breath and laughed until she cried. The release felt good in the midst of so much death and gloom.

CHAPTER THIRTY-FIVE

Gwen returned to her office and continued to go through the case files. She found two more that were suspect, although not as explicitly incriminating as the one found by CC.

Just before three p.m. CC returned, and Gwen couldn't resist putting her arms around her in a big bear hug. "How'd it go, hon?"

"I saw you laughing," CC pretended to pout. "Actually, it went really well. Doc Maynard is a gem. He's so gentle with the dead and he taught me so much. I don't think I'll ever be scared again, although it is a gruesome ordeal which I hope I don't have to go through again soon."

"That's great. He is a terrific man and a wonderful teacher. You can tell he loves his work," Gwen replied. "Did you find anything else that could help us in the investigation?"

"She chipped her tooth fairly recently, possibly when she fought her attacker. It would be great luck if we could find it at the murder site. The wounds were made with the same type of knife as with the others and were nearly identical to Meg's. This time Doc may have found flesh under her fingernails. We were thinking that she was able to fight harder than the others. In fact, Doc suggested maybe that's why he picked smaller women after killing Amy. The order of deaths appears to be Amy first, Meg second, Carole next and Reyna last."

"Tying Reyna's death into those of the others has been puzzling me," Gwen admitted. "The only thing I can think of is that she knew the other three, and our killer might have been worried she'd known enough from talking with them to go to the police."

"I still think Kathy's business partner, Linda, is at risk. Speaking of which, I should call and check with the officer assigned to her."

They'd barely started on the stack of files again when Scott returned. "It's a match." He beamed. "Sammy got the fibers from Wright's trunk and they're exactly what we expected. Better yet, he found a small amount of blood on the top of the trunk. It's out for DNA analysis."

"Even if it's inadmissible, I can't wait to get this information to the chief," Gwen said excitedly.

"Oh, and take a look at this," Scott said, holding up a small plastic bag.

"It's a piece of tooth!" CC exclaimed. "I'll just bet it was Amy's!"

"The chief is going to kill me." Gwen sighed. "We didn't have a search warrant for Wright's trunk."

Scott looked triumphant. "That's why I brought a copy of the disclaimer he signed for the repairs. It's fairly comprehensive and shows that Wright more or less left the car to be examined by authorized personnel. They use the same release for the cops to sign when they impound a vehicle and have it stored at Chuck's," Scott told her.

"This just might work!' Gwen said, as relieved as she was happy. "I'm going to see if I can see the chief now. Thanks guys!"

Gwen had to wait twenty minutes, but it was worth it to see the look on Chief Ziegler's face when she showed him all the evidence they had collected; the files she and CC had pulled to show conspiracy between the three men, the soccer game Brad had attended with Judge Garmer, Algier showing up with Garmer's bribe money, and Scott's suspicions that Algier would gladly pay to have lab results falsified. She thought he'd drop his teeth when she told him about the green fibers and piece of tooth found in Wright's trunk. Last but not least, and before he could utter a word about admissible evidence she showed him the disclaimer Wright had signed when he left his car at Chuck's.

"This is huge, Gwen. It's not just about a crooked ex-captain anymore. We're now talking about pressing charges against a judge and district attorney. I'm turning this all over to Internal Affairs," Chief Ziegler told her grimly.

"Does that mean we're off the case?" she asked anxiously.

"I'm sure they could use your help with many facets of this case. I'll have Fred Barzak meet with your team before the day is out to come up with a new strategy. He's a good guy, Gwen. I've worked with him for several years and have only the highest respect for his work."

"Okay, Chief," she conceded reluctantly. "I'll call everyone together and wait for him in my office."

"Thanks, Gwen. Whatever happens from here on in, this is terrific work. Let your team know how much I appreciate all their efforts."

"I will. Thanks."

Brad was already in Gwen's office when she returned. CC was still going through the files and had commandeered Scott into helping her with the remaining stack. Gwen let them know Chief Ziegler's decision and asked them all to be patient until they learned how Internal Affairs wanted them to proceed.

They chatted about the case and tried to envision three public servants scheming and plotting for their own benefit.

They all believed only Wright had been the perpetrator of the murders, but certainly the other two had been privy to some of his actions.

"May I interrupt?" A tall, handsome man in his late fifties knocked at the door. "I'm Fred Barzak."

"We've been expecting you, Mr. Barzak," Gwen said curtly, introducing herself and then her staff.

"Please, call me Fred. I've heard some very disturbing news," he said, closing the door behind him and taking a seat on the edge of Gwen's desk. "First of all, I want you to know that I'm not here to take anyone off the job. You've done outstanding work. All I'm asking is that you allow me and my team to assist you with some resources that you've not had at your disposal up to now."

"We can always use another pair of hands," Gwen said, softening.

"With the approval of the DA and our approved search warrants, I'm offering wiretaps, tracking devices for their automobiles, and video surveillance. You've done the groundwork and now we need to reel them in. Let them tell us in their own words and by their actions what they're up to," Fred told them.

"Now that's a bonus!" Scott said enthusiastically.

"Yeah, I like the way you think." Brad smiled.

"We would appreciate all the help you can give us," Gwen let him know. "What do you want us to do in the meantime?"

"I've read the reports you've given to Chief Ziegler, and I'd like you to continue doing the same things you've been doing. The only thing I disagreed with is Chief Ziegler's directive that you stay away from Captain Wright. I say, get in his face! The angrier you get him, the more likely he's going to make that incriminating call, or take off to a secret hiding place. And we'll be right there listening and watching when he does."

"How soon will you have the bugs in place?" CC asked.

"My team has already created minor disturbances to get the three men out of their way. My superiors have signed all the paperwork, so we have the green light. Right about now, Wright should be at his goddaughter's school finding her doing just fine after the nurse's mix-up about the child who was vomiting. Algier's wife had a minor fender bender and he is now on the scene talking to the officers, and poor Judge Garmer is stuck in the elevator at the courthouse for a few minutes. All tracking of their vehicles, phone bugs and video cameras, should be in place right about…" He picked up his cell phone. "Now."

CHAPTER THRITY-SIX

"I know you were pretty nervous about Internal Affairs taking over our investigation, but it turned out okay, didn't it?" CC asked, stroking Cashew who was sitting contentedly in her lap. She and Gwen had come home for dinner and a much needed break.

"Yeah, I was praying I would keep my cool. I was sure we were going to be tossed off the case, but it worked out great. I've heard nightmares about IA ripping the cases out of the investigative team's lap and screwing them up royally. But Fred seems like a pretty decent fellow."

"I heard somewhere that Barzak took over the position about two years ago and really cleaned house," CC remembered.

"Then I guess it's not like it used to be. I'm dying to see what he comes up with on the wiretaps. Those guys are the scum of the earth. There's nothing worse than a crooked cop." Gwen couldn't help but show her disdain.

CC nodded her agreement. "I nearly clapped my hands when he told us to get in Wright's face!"

"Yeah, that was great," Gwen agreed. "Let's just go to The Dive tonight and plan on visiting Tina's Pub tomorrow, okay? I think I've had enough drama for one day."

"Sure. That sounds good. You need to lighten up a bit though, hon. And I think I know just what you need," CC said impishly.

Gwen finally smiled. "We do have plenty of time."

***

Gwen felt determined as ever about the homicide cases as she drove to The Dive. Talking things over with CC had helped ease her mind and put her thinking back on track.

Gwen discovered when she arrived that most of the regulars hadn't heard about Amy's body being found. The press must not have picked up on it nearly as quickly as they had the others. Out of respect for Ben, she told him as delicately as possible. Jimmy and TJ were close enough to hear.

"Damn shame all them girls died for no reason," TJ said sadly.

"Sure would like to get my hands around the neck of whoever done them in," Jimmy agreed.

"Guess we kinda figured Amy wouldn't be found alive," Ben added, wiping a tear from his eye. "'Specially since the other two was already found dead."

"I just know the police have to be putting everything they've got into finding the killer, Ben. Mark my words, they'll get him," Gwen said soothingly.

"Won't bring 'em back though, will it? I miss them all. Like I said, my customers are my family."

"You have other family around here?" Gwen asked, trying to change the subject.

"Parents are long gone. My dad was a no-good rotten son of a bitch anyway. Beat up on my ma plenty. My mom was a saint…

went right up to heaven couple years back of cancer. I've got two brothers, but they split from these parts as soon as they could. I dunno, maybe went to the west coast. Haven't heard from them in years. Never even came back when Ma died. How 'bout you, Gwen?"

"I had one brother who died in the service. My dad died when I was a teenager, and Mom's in a nursing home…she has multiple sclerosis and is bitter about life in general, and especially toward me since my brother died. Like it was my fault he got blown up or something, I never could figure it out. I don't get out to see her very often. We weren't that close to begin with," Gwen admitted.

"You need to go see your mom, Gwen. Make peace before it's too late," Ben said softly.

"Yeah, I suppose. I will one of these days soon. I promise."

"There you go, girl! Now go beat some butt at that dart board."

"You got it."

CC was talking with some of the pool players and Gwen joined her when she was finished. They had another beer together, celebrating their progress on the investigation. It was nearly one a.m. when they arrived home, and were greeted by two very happy and perky dogs. They walked hand in hand to the park, talked, and let the dogs sniff every few feet of the way. After three a.m., they finally fell exhausted onto the bed and were asleep in each other's arms in a matter of minutes.

CHAPTER THIRTY-SEVEN

"You're into more of a routine than I am," CC stated the following morning over breakfast. "Are you going to have a difficult time moving to my place next week?"

"Excuse me?" Gwen almost choked on her coffee.

"Remember? We agreed to let the dogs get used to my place...one week with you, and then one week with me. I'm asking if you think you can adjust to staying at my place. It's a lot smaller, but it's cozy."

"CC, I'm head over heels for you. I hope you know that. I'd sleep outside in a dog kennel if it meant being with you."

"Like, what does that mean in English...head over heels?"

"It means I'm in love with you." Gwen got up and kissed CC tenderly. "Are you okay with that?"

"You know I've struggled with this. I didn't want it to happen like this...I mean so fast. But, I'm feeling the same way, Gwen. That's why I'm asking. It's been wonderful being with you this whole week, and I don't want to go home and be without you."

"That makes me the happiest woman in the world," Gwen said, kissing her again.

"We have a family and everything now with Peanut and Cashew. I know we can't keep moving back and forth every other week, so eventually we'll have to figure out something more permanent," CC continued.

"Any suggestions?" Gwen asked cautiously.

"Well, I've been pondering whether we should stay at your place or mine, and then it dawned on me. Why don't we look for another place? It would be ours, and not yours or mine."

"That's a great idea. I like it. We can start looking this weekend if you'd like," Gwen suggested.

"Yeah, it will be fun. I love to decorate, and I want a place big enough for each of us to have our own space. And of course, a fenced-in yard is a must," CC said, picturing her perfect house.

"And a white picket fence?" Gwen teased.

"Don't you just love those?" CC joked back.

"And gingerbread trim...just like in one of those fairytales we read as kids."

"Oh, I forgot...will Pierre be really upset? And what about Max?"

"I'm sure he'll be thrilled that he can finally buy me out. About six months ago, during one of our rare arguments where he was trying to hire me to do his laundry and cleaning, he mentioned that his sister would love to do all his domestic chores if she lived closer. And I'm sure we can invite Max over to visit Peanut and Cashew on occasion."

"Oh no, Gwen. He is such a...a MAN!"

Gwen laughed. "Yeah, that he is."

***

They all arrived at the precinct early at the request of Fred Barzak. The team was curious to find out what Barzak's team had found out in such a short period of time.

"Glad to see you're all here," Fred said, dropping a box of doughnuts on Gwen's desk. "Help yourselves."

"Thank you, Fred. How's it going with the surveillance?" Gwen asked, grabbing a powdered sugar doughnut.

"Very well. Better than expected, actually. We've confirmed your suspicions that Judge Garmer is getting paid off. Algier is the middle man, but appears to be on both sides of the fence. We discovered he is not only taking bribes, but extorting money and is heavily involved in the drug trade. They're blackmailing Wright for everything he's got. Garmer is trying to beef up his retirement savings. Wright's additional payoff for getting freed on bail is to find Garmer a nice, cozy condo off the Florida Keys. It shouldn't be any problem finding something through his sleazy contacts down there, but his cash account has been drained down to next to nothing. He's withdrawn over two hundred thousand in the past six months."

"Phew," Scott whistled. "That's some serious cash."

"So Wright's running scared?" CC asked.

"I'd be very surprised if he didn't try to disappear...leave the country...and hide in Mexico or the Caribbean very soon. Now that we have him monitored, he won't get very far. He won't be able to meet Algier's demands very much longer."

"So you think Garmer and Algier are onto him about the murders?" Brad asked.

"That's my guess, but nothing that explicit has come across on the surveillance yet," Fred told them. "One more thing. We found their meeting place. It's an abandoned warehouse not far from Tina's Pub. Algier sets up the meetings and lets Wright know when Garmer will be there to meet with him."

"A warehouse," Gwen mused. "Any chance that's where Wright murdered the women?"

"Good question. I'll let you know," Fred told her. "We haven't had time to search the premises, but I'll make it top priority."

"CC and I were going to pay another visit to Tina's today," Gwen told him. "Is that still a good idea?"

"By all means. I have a man working with Sammy around the clock in the area, so I don't think you need to worry about your safety. If Wright does show up and see that you're still nosing around, it may force him into making a quick decision. One way or another, it would be good to get him on tape talking about the women he killed. If it goes the other way, and causes him to try to go into hiding, we'll nab him and have plenty of time to interrogate him while he sits in prison," Barzak explained.

"And this time he won't have his team sitting by to pamper him," Scott said enthusiastically.

"Exactly." Fred smiled. "The loneliness and despair you experience in a prison setting, when all your so-called friends have quickly turned on you to save their own necks, does wonders for changing your tune."

***

Tina's was as deserted as it was the last time Gwen and CC had been there; the only other customer was one young man at the bar. The waitress was standing with her elbows resting comfortably on the bar and her hands on her cheeks, chatting with the man.

They chose the same table in the back as they had on their previous visit and waited patiently for the waitress.

She finally finished her conversation with the man and sauntered over. "Hey, I remember you. You're those two cops, aren't you?"

"Yes, we are," CC answered.

"You know, that man has come in a couple times since you were here, but he hasn't caused any more trouble. He always sits alone, has two cocktails, and leaves. I keep your card in my pocket," she said, pulling the crinkled business card from deep within her apron pocket. "Just in case."

"Thank you," Gwen said. "And the man hasn't met anyone else while he's here?"

"No. Not that I've seen. Of course, I have other customers to take care of. My feet and back are killing me by the time my shift is over. They have me watching the bar and the tables today.

I had to stock the shelves this morning, run back and forth from the kitchen for the breakfast crowd, and then start all over for lunch. Soon we'll be starting dinner and I've still got two more hours to work," she complained. "I'm Rosa, by the way."

"If it's not too much trouble, can we order a couple sandwiches?" Gwen asked.

"Oh, sure. The special today is roast beef on rye. It's very good. Served with cole slaw and potato salad."

Gwen looked at CC and she nodded. "We'll take two of those and two diet Cokes please."

"I thought I'd crack up in the middle of her tirade," CC whispered when Rosa had left to get their order.

"Yeah, me too," Gwen giggled. "I really don't think we can count on her observations. She seems awfully…how can I say this nicely…well, she seems awfully flaky, don't you think?"

"That's an understatement. I think the more politically correct word is 'wacko,'" CC laughed.

Rosa brought their drinks and said the sandwiches would be ready shortly. She then went back to the bar to resume her conversation with the young man. Gwen and CC chatted about the most important features they wanted to look for in a new house.

After twenty-five minutes, Gwen started getting annoyed. "How long does it take to slap together a couple of sandwiches?" she complained.

"I think Rosa forgot about us," CC admitted. "There are three of them now."

While they had been talking another man had come in, obviously a friend of the first. Rosa was talking animatedly with the two.

"I'll go find out what's happening with our lunch," Gwen said, but as she was starting to get up, Wright came in and sat with his back to them in the middle of the bar. "Uh, I think I'll wait."

They heard him call to Rosa and demand a drink. As before, he belted it down quickly and rudely asked for another. As she was serving his second beverage, Rosa happened to glance at them and a look of shocked recognition flashed on her face. It was obvious she finally remembered they were waiting to be served. Wright followed her gaze and turned to them with a look of astonishment. His expression quickly turned to rage.

"What the fuck…" He pulled away from the bar causing the barstool to come crashing down to the floor. Without stopping to right the stool, he strode quickly to their table. "You fucking cunts spying on me again?"

"Just having a bite to eat," Gwen said confidently.

"Three thousand places for 'a bite to eat' in this city, and you just happen to be here?" he said sarcastically. "I'm not buying it. What the hell do you want from me?"

"Nothing. Like I said, we're going to eat our sandwiches and leave. It's a free country. We can eat anywhere we chose," Gwen said, standing her ground.

"You fucking bitch. You'll be sorry you messed with me."

"Is that a threat?" CC asked.

"You're damn right it's a threat. I don't want to see you messing in my business again or I'll…I'll…" He paused.

"Kill me?" Gwen finished for him.

"The world would be a better place," he said and stalked off.

At the bar he slammed down his drink and left, leaving the barstool lying on the floor.

When Wright was gone, Rosa hurried to their table with their sandwiches. "I'm sorry it took so long," she apologized. "What's that guy got against two nice-looking women like you anyway?"

"Oh, he's just the cranky type," CC replied. "I don't think he likes women in general."

"He sure has an ax to grind against you," Rosa insisted. "You ex-lovers or something?"

Both CC and Gwen burst out laughing.

"I guess not, huh? Well, he sure has a temper and didn't leave a dime for a tip," Rosa said, storming over to the bar and setting the stool upright.

CHAPTER THIRTY-EIGHT

The Dive was deserted, so both CC and Gwen made it home shortly after ten p.m.

"This is the first time we've been home before midnight in the past two weeks," Gwen said happily.

"Let's watch a movie! We can cuddle on the couch with the boys!" CC suggested.

"Sure. You want to go for a walk with us first? Peanut and Cashew are kind of chomping at the bit here to get out," Gwen replied.

"I'll be with you as soon as I change into my sweats," CC answered. "Give me a minute."

Gwen put the leashes on the dogs and waited on the front porch for CC to get ready. Looking around, she noticed a dark car about a half block away, a figure sitting low in the driver's seat. She pulled the dogs back inside and grabbed her service weapon from the front closet, strapping it over her left shoulder under her jacket.

"I'm ready," CC said, bouncing out of the bedroom.

"We may have a bit of a problem. I think we're being watched, so let's take our guns in case we run into any trouble, okay?" Gwen said calmly so as not to get CC unduly rattled.

"You think it's Wright?" CC said, grabbing her weapon and shoving it in the waistline of her pants.

"I don't know. Could be."

"Best thing that could happen is if he tried to jump one of us and gave us cause to shoot. I'd love to wipe that evil smirk off his face once and for all," CC said with all the bravado she could muster.

"I know, but we both know that's not how we're going to handle him. We're good cops and play by the rules. Besides, we're still looking for answers. Killing him won't get us where we want him. Ready?"

"Yep."

They walked slowly down the block, stopping every few feet to let the dogs sniff the grass, and let the boys pee on the bushes and trees along the sides of the sidewalk. When they reached the park entrance, they noticed the dark car move forward. The windows were heavily tinted but they detected the shadow of only one person inside. It didn't look like he was going to get out and follow them, so they stepped up their pace and briskly walked the entire distance of the well-lit trail.

They reversed their path and headed back home. As Gwen was unlocking the front door, the car made a fast U-turn, sped up burning rubber, then raced quickly out of the neighborhood.

"Do you think he's just trying to scare us?" CC asked.

"Maybe. I'd better let Barzak know, just in case," Gwen said, pulling out her cell phone.

"I was expecting to hear from you," Fred announced, answering on the first ring.

"You saw the car following us?" Gwen asked.

"Yeah, we were further up the block. We followed Wright to your place after he left the warehouse," Barzak told her.

"He had a meeting at the warehouse with his buddies tonight?" Gwen asked.

"No, there was no meeting. Wright showed up like he was expecting someone else, but no one showed. He was noticeably angry when he left."

"We got him riled up at Tina's," Gwen told him, relating the scene he had caused and the threat he had made. "He had the fury of the devil in him when he left."

"Good. We've got him on the run. You shouldn't have to worry about him anymore tonight. Checkpoint three has him pulling into his garage," Barzak told her. "Someone will be stationed there to make sure he stays put."

"Okay, Fred. See you in the morning."

Gwen relayed everything to CC that Barzak had told her.

"I can't wait until he's locked up for good," CC said.

"I'm with you," Gwen agreed.

CC picked out the movie *Harry Potter and the Deathly Hallows* while Gwen made popcorn. Cashew jumped immediately on CC's lap, and Peanut snuggled close to Gwen's thigh as they cuddled together on the couch. All four were fast asleep before the movie was half over.

Sometime in the early morning hours, Gwen woke, turned off the TV and lights, and carried CC to bed. The dogs followed and nestled in at the foot of the bed as Gwen slipped in beside her.

***

At the precinct, Fred Barzak introduced them to Fritz Dietrich, one of his expert technicians. "Now Fritz is going to attach one of these tiny microphones to whatever you carry with you at all times. Most often we put them on purses, attaché cases, or even key chains. It's entirely up to you, but make sure you choose the item you keep with you all the time. The only place we prefer not putting them is on your guns. If you fired your weapon, it would blow the ears off the person monitoring the system," he said, drawing laughter from the team. "It may get dangerous from here on in, and I want to know where all of you are at all times. This has a tiny homing device. If you're in trouble, talk into it. You don't have to be right on top of it. The mike is so sensitive, you can be up to twelve feet away. Just talk normally if you need our assistance. You don't need to shout."

"But at home, I mean when I'm with my wife…" Scott mumbled, turning red.

"We're not going to invade your privacy," Barzak told them. "Whenever you're off duty and safely in your homes, call the command center and let them know. You can call them back when you're ready to have it turned back on. We've got someone monitoring twenty-four/seven."

"Phew." Scott let sighed and everyone laughed, causing him to redden again.

"I do want to alert you, in the event you are called out during your off hours, I will immediately have them activate your monitoring device. We've found that when someone is awakened for an emergency call or sudden sting operation, calling in is the farthest thing from their minds, so we do it for them," Barzak told them. "Scott, I'd rein in those raging hormones if I call you at home at two or three a.m.," he joked.

"Yes, sir," Scott said, sitting up straight and trying not to show his embarrassment.

All four chose their key chains and were rigged up to the command center within a matter of minutes.

"This is rather comforting, considering what happened last night," Gwen commented to Fred, then told the team about Wright spying on her at home.

"I finally got a return call from Linda," CC mentioned. "She's still feeling like someone is watching her, but is more comfortable about it now. It seems she stormed out of her house to confront a man sitting in his car down the street, and it turned out to be a plainclothes cop patrolling the area. They hit it off and she's now dating him!"

"Good for her," Brad laughed. "Fred, how soon do you think we can impound Wright's car? The lab sure would like to get their hands on more blood samples, if there are any. We've already confirmed the green fibers are definitely from his car, but the blood Sammy lifted was so miniscule, they can't do much with it."

"Give us a couple more days," Fred answered. "Oh, and I have a forensics team scheduled to scour the warehouse after our men are tucked away for the night."

"Can we join them?" Gwen asked hopefully.

"I'm afraid not. We're looking for every shred of evidence we can find, but we don't want to disturb anything. If we let them know we're onto the place, the men won't use it any longer. I'm still hoping we can get Wright, Algier and Garmer to conduct one of their meetings inside. We've installed some high-tech surveillance and would be able to playback any meeting they'd have like an Academy Award movie! I'm sure they'd all give us outstanding performances."

"Man, I'd sure like to see that!" Scott exclaimed.

"It may seem like the pace has slowed some, but it won't be long now," Barzak promised.

CHAPTER THIRTY-NINE

The following day the task force took the opportunity to clear their desks of other files requiring their attention. They made phone calls that needed to be returned regarding other pending cases that had been set aside as low priority. With the hectic pace the past couple of weeks, it was a welcome change. It was now a waiting game to see when Wright and his cohorts would make their next move.

Gwen and CC decided to skip going to The Dive and go home early to start packing for the move to CC's. At Barzak's suggestion that they keep the pressure on Wright and show him they weren't backing off because he had followed them, they planned on meeting at Tina's on the way home for a quick dinner. Thursday night's special was spaghetti and meatballs, and they were looking forward to a relaxing meal.

Gwen arrived at Tina's Pub first, around three thirty p.m. She came face-to-face with Wright and Algier as she entered. They were sitting at the bar having a heated discussion, but stopped talking the minute Gwen walked in. Wright looked like he wanted to strangle her, and Algier slapped a five-dollar bill on the bar and left without saying a word.

"Son of a bitch," Wright muttered and threw a few singles on the bar, hurrying out to follow Algier.

"Wright and Algier just left Tina's together," Gwen whispered into the microphone attached to her key chain.

Rosa was nowhere in sight and there was an older man tending bar. Gwen slid onto a stool and ordered a beer, waiting for CC. She arrived about twenty minutes later.

"You missed all the excitement," Gwen told her, recounting the scene with the two men.

"Sorry I missed it. I would have liked to watch Wright's face. Any reaction from Algier?"

"No. He was wearing his usual scowl, but didn't say a peep. Wright was more concerned with catching up to Algier than going off on another tirade. I sure hope Barzak is right and this case breaks wide open soon." Gwen sighed.

After CC got a beer they moved to one of the small tables. A short, pretty, well-dressed, older Hispanic woman came to their table shortly afterward to take their order.

"What happened to Rosa?" CC asked.

"She was fired yesterday. Bad attitude," the woman said in perfect English. "We've had several complaints about her rudeness and neglect of our customers. I hope you weren't treated badly. I'm Irma and my husband, Walter, is tending bar. We own this place. One of you wouldn't be looking for a job, would you?" she said, extending her hand.

Shaking her hand, Gwen replied, "No, but we'll sure check around and let you know if we think of anyone."

The spaghetti and meatball dinner was all you could eat, and came with garlic bread dripping in butter. They both ordered a second helping and stuffed themselves.

"I'm so full, I can't move," CC complained. "And I reek of garlic," she said, blowing her breath into her hand.

"No kisses for you. Yuck," Gwen laughed.

"You ate the same thing I did!"

"You're right. I couldn't resist kissing you, even with your icky bad breath."

She paid the bill and they were just on the way out the door when her cell phone rang.

"We're taking them down shortly, just as soon as all the warrants are signed," Barzak said. "Meet us at the precinct so we can make the assignments. We caught the three of them on tape, and they've just left the warehouse."

"We're on our way. Did Wright admit to the murders?" Gwen was anxious to find out.

"Let's just say Wright didn't argue when Algier told him he'd be acquitted for the murders. Algier made it perfectly clear what Wright still owed them, what it would gain him, and how he wanted it paid."

***

Barzak's small office was packed when Gwen and CC arrived, filled with task force members, Barzak's support staff, special operations marksmen and additional officers. Chief Ziegler had even showed up to take in the show.

As soon as everyone was seated, Barzak started playing the tape of the earlier meeting between Wright, Algier and Garmer. Just as Barzak had told Gwen, Algier told Wright that the two hundred thousand was just a down payment for destroying any evidence against him for the five murders. Wright insisted that Algier had killed Reyna, but Algier cut him off. Algier then demanded another three hundred thousand and the condo in the Florida Keys if Wright wanted to walk as a free man. Wright's protests that he couldn't come up with the money fell on deaf ears, and as soon as Algier was finished making the demands Garmer left the warehouse as quickly as he'd entered.

Wright tried gaining sympathy with Algier, but Algier only sneered, and told him he'd better come up with the funds if he expected to live. Wright grabbed Algier by the jacket, and Algier roughly shrugged him off, pushing him onto the floor. Algier then made a mocking gesture, pretending to shoot Wright, laughed wickedly, turned and left.

The tape ended with Wright standing up and brushing himself off with shaking hands, clearly a broken and defeated man.

"That, my friends, is sufficient evidence to put these three away for good," Barzak stated over the cheers of the men and women in the room.

Barzak then assigned Gwen, Brad and Scott as the leads, with two of his staff and one additional officer, making three teams of four. "There are extra bulletproof vests in the corner, if you don't have your own. Gwen, your team is assigned to bringing in Wright. Brad, you're responsible for Garmer, and Scott, you'll take down Algier. CC, you, I and the rest of the team members will split up into twos and block all entrances and exits to the suspects' residences as soon as the teams let us know they're in position. Any questions?"

When no one said anything, Barzak said, "Okay, people. Let's go get 'em. Good luck and be safe!"

***

Brad's team arrived first, and as soon as their backup was in place, Garmer was arrested without incident. As Brad fastened his handcuffs on Garmer's wrists and read him his rights, Garmer was trying to explain to him that there was a misunderstanding which he could easily clear up when he arrived at the precinct. The man was so confident he was above the law, if he was the least bit upset, he didn't let it show.

Scott's team moved in on Algier, and had to use a battering ram to break down the front door after Algier barricaded himself behind it. The man was belligerent and combative, but was subdued quickly by three of the team members. Scott moved in behind and cuffed him, read him his rights, and helped drag the man to the waiting police van. Algier continued to berate the officers the entire way to the precinct, as if the tongue-lashing he gave his captors could possibly help his situation.

As Gwen and her team slid out of the police van with their weapons drawn, she felt the whoosh of a flying bullet whiz past her right ear before it crashed into the side of the van with a deafening clang. Everyone immediately dropped into a crouching position and moved behind the vehicle. *Bang, bang, bang, bang,* Gwen counted the bullets as Wright unloaded his pistol into the van and ground nearby. He had one shot left before he would have to reload, so she picked up a rock and threw it as hard as she could. It bounced on the porch and crashed against the side of the railing, before stopping with a dull thud. *Bang.* Wright fired toward the sound. Gwen motioned to one of the officers and they ran as fast as they could, each taking one side of the house. The other two followed suit as soon as they saw that Gwen and her partner had made it safely, standing straight and rigid against the outside walls.

Gwen inched her way toward the back of the house and assessed the back entryway. There was no screen door, so they had just one wooden door to get through. It was doubtful Wright could cover both the front and the back door at the same time, so she spoke into her microphone to the backup unit, "I need you to keep Wright occupied in the front of the house. Keep firing toward the porch, but keep your shots low. I want to take him alive."

"Units one and two have already transported their subjects. We're on our way to assist," she heard Barzak say.

"We can use all the help we can get," Gwen muttered to herself.

As she rounded the corner and crept toward the door, the young marksman on the other side also moved around the opposite corner to the back of the house. He nodded, indicating he was moving toward the door, backing her up. She moved slowly and ducked low to get past the window. When she got within a foot of the door, she reached out and tried the doorknob. It was locked.

The marksman put his hand out to indicate for her to stop. He pulled a black leather case from his pocket and extracted a slender tool. Then moving forward, he knelt close to the door, put the point of the tool below the doorknob and a couple seconds later moved away and straightened up. He nodded.

When she tried the doorknob a second time it turned easily. Two more figures rounded the corner. It was Barzak and another one of the sharpshooters. Barzak held up three fingers and started counting down. As they stormed through the door, there was a flurry of firepower. They scrambled to duck behind the dining room chairs and one of the marksmen kicked over the kitchen table, ducking behind it for cover. As Gwen dove for cover, she felt a powerful blast pushing her back. She grabbed her left shoulder with her right hand, and when she brought it back down it was covered with blood.

When she glanced back up, Barzak was at her side. The shooting had stopped, but the room was filled with smoke so she couldn't see past the doorway leading out of the kitchen. The two marksmen were already on their feet, guns pointed ahead of them as they crept through the smoke and into the other room.

"Take it easy," Barzak whispered. "Let them take care of it." He took off his jacket and pressed it firmly on Gwen's shoulder, trying to staunch the flow of blood.

It seemed like an eternity, but only a few minutes had passed until one of the agents returned.

"He's still alive, but barely. Tried to take his own life, but just grazed the side of his head. He took one of our bullets to his neck and another to the abdomen."

Gwen listened as if she was far, far away. Her body seemed to be floating away to a distant, very peaceful place. She lost consciousness just as the rest of the crew entered the house.

CHAPTER FORTY

"You're not going anywhere," CC insisted.

"Come on, hon. I feel fine," Gwen begged.

"The doctor said you need to rest for at least a week, and it's only been two days," CC said exasperated. "You lost a lot of blood, Gwen."

"I haven't done anything for the past two days, and I'm going to go stark raving mad if I don't get out for some fresh air. You can drive," Gwen insisted.

"Well…" CC was thinking it over.

Gwen had a cast on her arm from her shoulder to the tips of her fingers. After four hours of surgery to repair the torn tendon, the doctors felt she had a good chance of recovering fully.

Wright was still hanging in there, and as of today, his chances of recovery were about fifty-fifty. One of the detectives guarding his hospital door said he was starting to talk in his sleep. He was sure he'd be up and trying to escape any day now. The hospital staff didn't quite agree.

"Help me get my shirt on and let's go!" Gwen said anxiously.

"Just be careful and let me do it! Geez, woman. You are stubborn!" CC finished helping Gwen dress, grabbed the Scarletsville street map and they were off.

***

The third house they looked at was beautiful, though a few thousand more than they had planned on paying. The yard was fully enclosed with chain-link fencing, and the far end had several mature apple trees. The house was aluminum-sided in light beige, and all the trim was painted hunter green. Inside the rooms were sunny, with a huge bay window in the family room overlooking the backyard. All the walls had a fresh coat of beige paint. There were four bedrooms, with a full bathroom off the master bedroom. Two of the bedrooms were smaller, and had another bathroom between the two. The kitchen and dining rooms were spacious and modern. The living room was huge and had a built-in fieldstone fireplace.

"I can see a bear rug in front of the fireplace," Gwen mused.

"We could each decorate one of the smaller bedrooms and have our own den or workroom," CC said excitedly.

"This is perfect," Gwen agreed. "I wonder if they'd accept an offer for less than the asking price."

"It wouldn't hurt to try," CC urged. "Let's do it as soon as we get home!"

CHAPTER FORTY-ONE

Chief Ziegler smiled when he saw Gwen. "I didn't expect to see you back so soon."

"I'm feeling a whole lot better," she said.

"You've been released for full duty? I need a doctor's release before you can come back to work," he said firmly.

"Well...uh, I feel well enough. I saw my doctor yesterday, and I'm released from complete bed rest. Brad called and said Wright is going to make it, so I figured I'd give them a hand with the paperwork. I promise I won't do anything strenuous," Gwen begged.

"You know the rules as well as I do, Gwen. I believe you that you're feeling better, but you still need to rest. If you overdo it now, it will take longer for your full recovery. I need you back here, but when you're one hundred percent," Ziegler told her.

"I was just…"

"No. That's an order," Ziegler interrupted her plea. "Give it another few days, see your physician again, and we'll talk then about putting you back full time. It's for your own safety."

"I know. It's hard to be out of the loop. I miss my team," Gwen said resignedly.

"I know. You're young and strong, so I don't doubt you'll be running another marathon with your crew soon. Just enjoy the time off while you can, and we'll see you back here in a few days."

***

Gwen's mood brightened dramatically when she arrived home and checked her e-mails. The owner of the house they'd bid on accepted their offer. She called her agent and got the ball rolling. If all went well, the closing would take place in six weeks and they could move in shortly thereafter. Pierre was anxious for her to move, having readily agreed on the price for him to buy her out. CC's house still was up for sale, but she had two potential buyers; they were waiting to see if the bank would approve their financing.

Gwen tried to call CC to tell her the good news, but was told she was "who knows where" in the building. After a long nap, she woke up at three p.m. and got busy with her dinner preparations. She was about to burst with excitement by the time CC came home at four.

"Wow, this is a nice surprise," CC smiled, giving Gwen a kiss and hug. "Those steaks looked wonderful."

"I've got a little surprise for you." Gwen tried to hide her excitement.

"Hmm…you must be feeling better. I've been wondering how soon we could get romantic again," CC said, nestling into Gwen's arms.

"That too," Gwen said, kissing her passionately.

"Too?" CC asked. "What am I missing?"

"I found out this morning that our offer on the new house was accepted. We should close in six weeks!"

"That's great!" CC screamed. "I'm so excited!"

"Careful, I don't need a broken eardrum." Gwen laughed. "I'm excited too."

"You could have called me at work to let me know." CC pretended to be mad.

"I tried, but they said you were gallivanting all over the building," Gwen protested.

"I certainly was not! Brad, Scott and I are working with Fred to finish detailed reports on everything that happened during the investigation. Now that it looks like Wright will be able to stand trial, we don't want to miss anything."

"I'm sorry I'm not able to help you guys," Gwen said sadly.

"We've incorporated all your notes. Even Fred was impressed with how thorough you were with the documentation. I think we have everything we need, but I'll bring home the final draft when we're done so you can read through it."

"I'd appreciate that," Gwen said, brightening. "I see the doctor tomorrow. I'm hoping they take this damn cast off my arm. It itches like crazy!"

"I know you've been uncomfortable, but it shouldn't be too much longer. And I want to get professional movers so you don't strain your shoulder. Oh, Gwen! I can't wait to make our new home together. This is so exciting."

"Me too. And I'm famished. Let's eat!"

***

Another week went by before Gwen was able to have her cast removed, and was finally released to go back to work on light duty. During the last days of her time off, she was able to get all the paperwork completed, signed and notarized to purchase their new home. CC accepted an offer on her home, and Gwen was able to handle everything for her. It seemed to CC like every night Gwen had an exhausting amount of paperwork for her to read and sign.

By the time Gwen started back to work, they were all being called daily for meetings with the district attorney and prosecuting team. Every detail of their case against Wright, Algier and Garmer was carefully scrutinized and it was decided which member of the team would testify to each of the charges. As lead of the task force, Gwen would be testifying for the majority of the complaints filed against the men, but CC, Brad and Scott would also be called to testify. Fred's team was still compiling evidence as they processed items found in the residences and autos of all three men. They had also found the room where Wright had slaughtered the women. It was a small office in the back of the warehouse. Spraying Luminal over the cinderblock walls and cement floor had provided them with plenty of blood splatters to be analyzed. There was some blood pooled under a table and near metal filing cabinets that hadn't been cleaned at all. A wooden block of kitchen knives taken from Wright's home most likely contained the butcher knives used on the women. Wright's fingerprints were everywhere. The number of items confiscated was overwhelming, and each had to be labeled, categorized and thoroughly evaluated. Each memo, e-mail, and phone conversation recorded needed to be grouped with related items to fill in the blanks and tell the entire incriminating story of the men's complicated and corrupt practices. Based upon the sheer volume of evidence, District Attorney Fellerman requested that all three men be tried together, so that their efforts would not be duplicated, but the defense disagreed and was arguing for separate trials.

In the evenings, Gwen and CC packed boxes and discarded things they didn't need. Every morning on the way to the precinct they stopped at a donation center to drop off boxes of clothing and household items that were too good to be thrown away. With two residences to pack, they had their work cut out for them, but with the two of them working together they were making good progress.

CHAPTER FORTY-TWO

When Stanley Wright was well enough, he was transferred to the infirmary at the Wisconsin State Correctional Facility. He was mobile only with the use of a wheelchair, but at least could move from the infirmary and access the prison's law library during the one-hour periods prisoners were allotted for free time. He came up with an elaborate plan to countersue the state for wrongful imprisonment, and he would accuse Garmer and Algier for masterminding the entire scheme. He was still working on figuring out how to finagle the evidence to implicate Algier in all the murders. He needed to contact someone who could get into the police evidence room and exchange some of the evidence. He had some ideas as to who he would recruit. There were plenty of cops he had worked with who would willingly volunteer to do a small favor, if the price was right.

Wright contacted his attorney, Jordan Bell, who met him in the prison cafeteria. It took Wright nearly forty-five minutes to tell Bell how he wanted to be represented, and confided in him regarding the additional false evidence that would be found to turn the suspicion away from him and incriminate Algier.

When he was finished outlining his plan, Bell said, "Stanley, I've known you a long time. You and I go way back...we were young men when we first met. But you've chosen a path I took an oath to never go down. I have a reputation to maintain and a family who's proud of the man I am. I'm not willing to throw away my morals for any man. I can't represent you any longer."

"What do you mean? You can't drop me! I paid you good money to represent me against the claims I killed my daughter."

"Things have changed, Stanley. This mess you're involved in goes way beyond killing your daughter in an insane rage. I read through the formal complaint, and you've broken the law, and the sacred trust bestowed upon a public official, in just about every way that could possibly be imagined. I don't know what possessed you to go this route, but I certainly cannot condone it. In fact, I won't be any part of it. That's final, Stanley. No further discussion," Bell said sternly, getting up to leave.

"But, you're my friend. I'll work it your way...just don't abandon me," Wright whined.

"No, Stanley. I can't. I'm sorry." Bell left quickly without another word.

***

Judge John Garmer had a lot of favors to call in, or so he thought. He spent hours of his free time leaving messages for those he had helped in the past. He became increasingly infuriated as his calls were ignored. Over the years he had reduced the charges or forced acquittals for dozens of his friends and colleagues, and now that he needed a little help, they wouldn't give him the time of day.

Out of desperation, he finally called two of the best defense lawyers he'd witnessed representing the toughest cases in his courtroom. He knew the price would be steep, but staying in prison was a fate worse than death. He needed fresh air and freedom. He was presently sequestered from the general prison population because of his position, having sentenced many of the inmates to their present status, but he still didn't feel safe. He doubted the guards gave a damn whether he was protected or not. He kept to himself as much as possible, but there were always occasions where he could be at risk of attack. He was alone in his cell, but was required to eat his meals in the cafeteria and shower once a week with the general populace. The only thing keeping him sane was his thoughts of freedom.

Brian Jacoby and Carl Washington finally agreed to take his case. The two defenders were as different as night and day, but were the toughest lawyers in the city. Garmer knew part of their reasoning for representing him was the high-profile nature of this case, but they weren't coming cheap either. Not that the money bothered him—he'd stashed plenty away in foreign accounts under assumed names. If only he hadn't gotten quite so greedy, and quit just a little sooner. He already had a sweet little woman waiting for him in a Swiss chalet located in the Alps. He'd promised her he was retiring at the end of the year to be with her.

Brian Jacoby was short, dark and compact. He had recently represented the Jewish Defense League in the Midwest region, and rarely lost a case. Carl Washington was black as coal, and looked like a professional football linebacker. The man had a brilliant mind and easily swayed juries over to his side with his easygoing banter and deep melodic voice. If anyone could win his case, it was these two men.

**

District Attorney Lawrence Algier was probably in the toughest spot of the three accused. In his position as middleman, he more often made enemies with his contacts, rather than foster friendships. Although he'd made a lot of money over the years, he also had expensive habits. He had lavished his girlfriends with expensive jewelry and fine dining, had been an impeccable dresser, and his hobbies included piloting his own jet and sailing expensive yachts. Traveling the world at every opportunity, he'd been to Europe, traveled extensively in the Mideast, been in every port in South America and had most recently been on an African safari. He didn't believe in saving for the future, as he lived for the moment. In his line of work, the future was uncertain and the risks were many. Therefore, he was left working with a public defender. His chances of getting off were slim, but he agreed to testify against the others and accept a plea bargain to keep his sentence to a minimum. He could easily pick up the pieces and start over after a few years of serving time. He wasn't worried.

CHAPTER FORTY-THREE

At last, one of Garmer's contacts returned his call. Garmer had been stewing, anxious to put his plans in motion, and finally this man made Garmer a very happy man. He knew that this contact could do the job required, and although his price was steep, Garmer didn't give the money a second thought. It was a perfect plan, and now it would be finished within a few short days.

His contact, a guard at the prison, had been to see Garmer many times during his time on the bench. He was a decent man, but had two sons who were constantly getting into serious trouble and had been arrested several times. They both should be serving long prison sentences by now, but they remained on the streets, free men, thanks to Garmer. Sure, he had accepted payment of several thousand dollars over the years, but that was only a formality in doing business. Oh yes, this man owed Garmer plenty, and he would soon collect on the guard's debt.

Not wanting to say anything over the phone, the man agreed to visit Garmer in his cell later in the day.

***

Wright pushed his food around the plate, not feeling at all well this morning. He wasn't hungry, and it wasn't just the crap they served for meals here that made him ill. He had stomach cramps and was lightheaded.

As he sat feeling sorry for himself, he felt a looming presence behind him. A white man, well over six feet tall and with a shaved head sat down beside him. His huge arms were covered with tattoos.

"They took Algier out," the man said softly, shoving scrambled eggs into his mouth.

"Huh?" Wright didn't understand what the man had said.

"Algier. Gone."

Wright just looked at the man with a blank expression. With a look that mocked Wright's ignorance, he motioned to the television bolted to the wall. The headline news showed a man being carried out of the prison with a white sheet covering his body. The announcer was saying that Lawrence Algier had been found dead in his cell this morning with a broken neck. There were no witnesses and they were investigating his death.

Wright turned away from the TV, vomited on his plate, and passed out. He fell out of his chair and hit the floor with a heavy thump.

***

"He's been bleeding internally for a few days. We caught it in time, but he'll need a few days bed rest before he's transferred back to the prison," the doctor was telling Gwen and Fred.

"So he's not critical?" Gwen asked.

"Well, there's always a chance for infection with these kinds of injuries. The tear is in the upper intestine, which holds a great deal of bacteria. But, we were able to clean out the area as well as possible. I think he'll make it just fine."

"Is he conscious?" Fred wanted to know.

"He's still groggy from the anesthesia, but he's awake now. You can have ten minutes with him. No more."

"Thank you, Doctor," Gwen said.

Wright looked terrible, Gwen thought as they entered his room. He looked like he had lost as much as fifty pounds since she had seen him last.

He glanced up and said softly, "I'm a dead man."

"The doctor says you'll recover fully," Barzak told him.

"No. That's not what I'm talking about. Soon as I leave this hospital, Garmer will have me killed just like Algier."

"How do you know Garmer was responsible for Algier's death?" Barzak asked.

Wright squinted at the man through droopy eyes and said, "Give me a break. Isn't it obvious?"

"We can offer you protection if you talk," Barzak told him. "But no bullshit and I want to know everything."

Wright closed his eyes and sighed. "Maybe. I'll think about it."

"We'll be back," Barzak advised.

Wright was asleep by the time they were out the door.

"Do you think he'll really come clean?" Gwen asked.

"What does he have to lose? Like he said, he's a dead man either way you look at it. Either the judge gets to him or we crucify him in court. I'm sure he knows by now that we can tie him to the murders of Meg, Carole and Amy from the evidence found at the warehouse. My guess is that he planned to go back and clean up his mess, but we nabbed him before he got around to it. I would think that he'd be anxious to cut a deal."

"I sure hope you're right. The evidence against him is overwhelming," Gwen agreed. "I just want to know why. Do you think Garmer will ever be charged for Algier's murder?"

"Probably not. The guards are very tight-lipped and protect their own. It's an entirely different community and way of life inside the prison walls. The guards and inmates have an unspoken code of conduct that's pretty hard to penetrate. I sometimes think that the more seasoned thugs have more governing power than the administration."

"I've heard that opinion expressed before," Gwen replied.

"I'm sure Judge Garmer will lose his position, but without the testimony of Algier, the conspiracy charges won't stick. All we have is circumstantial evidence on him. Remember, he let Algier do all the talking. He's hired some high-powered attorneys and I'm sure he won't spend another day in prison after the trial."

"That sucks," Gwen said sadly.

"At least we got Wright off the streets. He's the most dangerous of the three in my opinion," Fred mused. "People want to pay bribes and deal drugs, it would take an army of officers a hundred times the size of our department to clean up just the city of Scarletsville. It's the cold-blooded killers I'm most thankful that we're shutting down."

Gwen had to agree. "I suppose so."

***

The following day, at Wright's request, Fred and Gwen paid him another visit at the hospital.

"If I talk, what's in it for me?" Wright asked gruffly.

"I talked to the DA and he's agreed not go for the death penalty if you come clean. You'll get a life sentence for each of the murders with no parole. Best I could do," Barzak told him.

"Concurrent, not consecutive?" Wright asked. If they agreed to concurrent sentences, where each year of time served would count for each sentence, he might be able to make parole before his eightieth birthday. If the sentences were consecutive, one ending and the next starting, he'd be dead long before his time was served.

"Give me a minute," Barzak said, taking his cell phone out to the hallway.

When he returned, he told Wright, "The DA will consider concurrent sentences only if you leave no holes in your testimony. You'll answer every question completely and honestly."

"Agreed," Wright said quickly.

"Start from the beginning," Barzak demanded, after placing a tape recorder on the bedside table and stating the names of the people present in the room.

"I got tied up with the judge...uh, that's Garmer...when I was trying to nail some thugs bringing in illegal merchandise from Mexico. Garmer liked my style, and had me contact Algier. Garmer always had me work through Algier, who said he'd cut a deal for my informants, and we'd partner up and take a cut in the illegal trade. They wanted in on a little business I had going in Florida too, and I thought what the heck. It was getting to be more than I could handle myself anyway. I said I'd be okay with anything as long as it didn't involve drugs. About that time my daughter had started using and we argued about it all the time. I honestly tried everything I could think of to get her back on the straight and narrow. She was such a sweet girl when she was clean," Wright said with tears in his eyes.

"Anyway," he continued, "someone told Kathy about some of my illegal dealings. I figured it was Algier, 'cause the money was coming in real slow. She was pretty strung out from the drugs and yelling at me, and I grabbed her from that fleabag they were using and took her home. Honestly, I wouldn't...I didn't intend to hurt her. But she kept yelling and came after me with a metal bookend, and when I tried to defend myself, well...the rest is history."

"Then you killed four more women after that. Why?" Gwen demanded.

"They were all on drugs and were feeding them to my little girl. I'd been following Kathy for several months before she died," he admitted.

"None of those girls were using or dealing drugs," Gwen said angrily.

"But I saw them handing Kathy packages! I've got pictures," Wright protested.

"Meg and Kathy were going to be business partners. I'd imagine that the packages you saw pass between them were the legal documents we found at your daughter's apartment. Carole was giving Kathy motorcycle magazines and advising her on the purchase of a used one, and I'm sure the relationship between Kathy and Amy was just as innocent."

"Oh no." Wright covered his eyes and wept. When he had composed himself he said, "There were more on my hit list, but I never was able to get them alone. Somebody got Kathy's drugs for her, and I was bound and determined to see them suffer like she did. I chose the people she saw most often as the first ones I went after. I guess I chose wrong."

"Yes, I guess you did," Gwen snarled. "The crosses…what was the significance of that?"

"I grew up in a devout Catholic family. I was even an altar boy as a young man." He smiled, reliving the memory. "It's been years since I stepped foot into a church, but I did remember that God is forgiving. I held a ceremony after each of the murders, lighting candles and praying, atoning for the sins of the women and asking Him to forgive me."

"That's sick," Gwen couldn't help herself from saying out loud.

"What about Reyna?" Barzak asked.

"That was Algier's idea. She knew far too much from talking to all the other women, and she had seen him and Garmer together at The Dive one afternoon. He was sure she was putting two and two together. Besides, he felt it would throw the investigators off-kilter if someone like her was murdered. He ordered me to accompany him, and we decided not to move the body after I stabbed her. She was too heavy, and why even bother trying?"

"You are one sick man, Captain," Barzak said in disgust.

"It's odd," Wright said with a smirk and faraway look on his face. "You think you wouldn't be able to hurt anyone if your life depended on it. Then after the first one it gets easier. The power is overwhelming and you start liking it. It's addictive. Had I not gotten caught, I would have killed every drug dealer in the city."

"And taken a lot of innocent lives with them," Gwen stated without hiding her loathing for Wright.

"The bad for the good of all. We're all going to die sooner or later anyway," Wright answered.

"I'm glad you'll never have the opportunity again to play God," Gwen said softly. "It's not becoming to you at all."

CHAPTER FORTY-FOUR

"Are you already packed and ready to go?" Gwen asked impatiently.

"Yep, just got to get the boys in their carriers," CC answered.

The case was finally wrapped up, and the women had taken a week of much-needed vacation. They were finally going to spend three days at the Wisconsin Dells. Gwen was going to keep the promise she had made to Ben when she and the bartender at The Dive had talked about their families. They planned to visit her mother on the way.

On the weekend after their return from the Dells, they had invited CC's family for a visit. The Carpenter family reunion would be fun, and they had purchased cots and sleeping bags to accommodate CC's four brothers and two sisters. They were giving the master bedroom to her parents, and would move into the guest room.

In the meantime, Wright's plea agreement had been accepted without a hitch, and he was now safely tucked away in the Wisconsin State Prison for a minimum of thirty-five years. As he had calculated, he would be well into his eighties if he ever made parole. That a parole board would ever consider his release was doubtful, but stranger things had happened within the justice system.

Garmer's high-powered attorneys had come through. He had been fined one hundred thousand dollars and set free. Last anyone had heard, he was enjoying retirement in the Florida Keys. His new condo was on a golf course overlooking the Atlantic Ocean, and he was quickly forming new alliances. The Scarletsville police weren't worried, as long as he abided by the court order barring him from returning to Wisconsin.

Life was good for Gwen and CC. Each day their love and respect for each other was strengthened, and they were both happy with their commitment to spend their future together. Their home radiated love and warmth, and Peanut and Cashew brought so much fun and laughter to their lives, they had added two kittens to the family. They were considering another larger dog, but hadn't found the perfect matchup for their little ones yet.

"Hey, is it going to be in this lifetime?" Gwen came up behind CC and gave her a hug. When she turned to reply, Gwen kissed her passionately.

"You keep that up, we'll never get out of here," CC threatened.

"You know what I love about our relationship? Well, one of the things anyway—I can never get enough of you, CC. The more I'm with you, the more I learn about you, the more I want to be with you."

"I'd say that's pretty cool. I feel the same way," CC said seriously.

"Come on, I'll help you get the dogs settled in the car." Gwen smiled. "Take my hand and we'll go riding off into the sunset."

"Gwen, it's just barely past nine in the morning!"

"I know, but it sounded good, didn't it?" Gwen laughed. "I love you!"

"I love you, too. Let's go!"

Bella Books, Inc.

Women. Books. Even Better Together.

P.O. Box 10543
Tallahassee, FL 32302

Phone: 800-729-4992
www.bellabooks.com